Feral
DRAGON

EARTH DRAGONS BOOK 5

CHARLENE HARTNADY

CHAPTER 1

S tone knocked again.

Still no answer. Weird. Maybe he'd gotten the date all wrong. *No!* He was sure he hadn't. Just to be certain, Stone pulled his phone out of his pocket. No messages. He scrolled through his correspondence with Sand from the week before. *Yep!* Just as he had thought. This was the right date. The right time. The right place. He knocked again, feeling dread. *Shit!* He was an idiot. He looked down at the neatly wrapped package in his hands. A colossal idiot. What had he been thinking when he decided to buy this? Maybe he could quickly leave and ditch the thing. It didn't seem like anyone was home anyway.

Stone was just turning away from the door when Sand appeared looking grim-faced. His friend ushered Stone into the hallway before closing the door behind them.

Crap! This was bad. It was supposed to be a celebration. "Oh shit!" Stone mumbled. "Is this what I think it is?"

Sand looked at the closed door for a beat before widening his eyes, which were bloodshot. "Sorry, I should have called to warn you. It's been a bit… emotional here today."

"I take it…" Stone pushed out a breath, "things didn't work out as planned." He wanted to hide the gift—which was burning holes in his hands—behind his back.

Sand ran a hand through his already unruly hair. "We were so sure," he whispered. "So sure it would work this time."

"I know. The human healer said that Macy would be highly fertile after the surgery. What happened? I mean, this was supposed to be 'it.' You've been trying for months. How many heats has it been now? All the drugs and scans—"

"I know. I know," he muttered, raking his fingers through his hair again. "I tried to warn Mace. Tried to keep myself from getting too hopeful as well, but… we let ourselves get carried away in the end. We even started talking like… like Macy was pregnant already. That the test would be just a formality. You know that since you've heard us do it."

Stone nodded. He certainly did. The package in his hands suddenly felt like it was covered in flashing neon lights.

"The babies this and the babies that," Sand went on. "Mace even said she felt pregnant. Tender breasts and nausea. The whole nine yards."

"That does make it worse to swallow. No wonder she's taking it so hard. When did you find out?"

"A few hours ago. The pregnancy test she took yesterday was negative but that doesn't mean anything. We couldn't wait, so I took her to see our doctor this morning." He rubbed his face with his hand, looking exhausted.

"I can guess the rest."

"Yeah well, I can't take it when Mace cries. It kills me. I want her happy. I would do anything for her but in this, I'm helpless. There's nothing I can do." His shoulders slumped in defeat.

"You're a fantastic mate to your female. You are doing everything in your power. More importantly, you are here for her every step of the way," Stone reminded him.

"She's so afraid I'll leave her one day if she doesn't become pregnant." Sand shook his head, his jaw tight.

"No way. I don't think I've ever seen a male more enamored than you. As you said, it's an emotional process. It obviously makes her feel vulnerable."

"I know. She also really wants children. She always has," Sand explained.

"It's tough." Stone paused. "All you can do is be there for her. Keep telling her how much she means to you. Also, you guys have only been trying for a few months. It's early days."

"A few months is a long time considering I'm a non-human. Most females become pregnant first time every time."

"That's true, but Macy isn't most females. She has very definite problems. You need to remember that."

"Endometriosis is no joke." Sand shook his head. "I just wish she would stop being so hard on herself. We do have time. If she doesn't become pregnant on the next heat, I think we should stop trying for a while. It's getting more and more emotional each time. Mace takes it harder and harder. I want to take a break."

"That's a catch twenty-two though." Stone frowned. "I thought your doctor said that the older she gets, the worse her chances are."

"Britt… Doctor Baker did, but you must also remember that the longer Macy is mated to me the better her body will become at healing itself. The better her senses will become. As you know, it is a natural phenomenon. We need to give that a chance to kick in as well. Mace might improve without medical intervention. It could happen on its own. I've tried telling her that, but she's just so single-minded right now. I hate seeing her like this."

"I'm sure. I'll leave you guys to—"

"Mace insisted that you still come over. She's prepared your favorite meal. You know how she worries about you as well."

Stone frowned. "Are you sure? I don't mind giving you some time to yourselves. And she should stop worrying so much. Most males around here don't have a mate." He chuckled.

"Most males around here have family. You don't." Sand looked solemn.

He felt an ache in his chest.

His friend smiled. "You have us though. When we arranged dinner, we agreed it would be to celebrate or to commiserate, remember? We'll have some wine and enjoy some good food. It'll do Macy good. It'll do you good too."

Stone winced. "We need to do something with this." He held up the box he was holding. The one wrapped in pretty paper. "I guess you guys weren't the only ones with high hopes."

"Oh…" Sand rubbed his chin. "Baby stuff?"

Stone nodded. "I realize now that it was a really bad idea."

"I'll take care of it. Come in." Sand took the box from him. He hid it in the back of the closet by the door. "There."

"Thank you." Stone nodded.

They went inside. Macy smiled when she saw him. She was holding a glass of white wine. "Hey." She smiled even more brightly, but her eyes were red-rimmed and puffy. He could see that she'd used make-up to try to cover up.

"Hey… um…" He looked down at his feet before looking back at her. "Sand mentioned… the bad news…"

Her face dropped and her lip quivered.

"I just wanted to say how sorry I am."

"Thanks." Her voice hitched.

Sand put his arm around her, squeezing her hip. "What can I get you to drink?"

"Beer would be good. I can get it…" He gestured towards the kitchen.

"No sweat." Sand went to fetch his drink.

"You didn't bring a date tonight?" Macy asked, changing the subject.

He made a face. "I never bring a date, Mace, yet you ask me every time." He chuckled.

"I know." She smiled. "That's why I'm asking. I keep telling you to bring someone and you never do."

He shrugged. "I haven't met anyone I want to spend time with."

"Are you going on the hunt this weekend? Maybe

then…" She raised her brows, her eyes brightening up.

"Nah!" He shook his head. "I've been on a couple of those things but," he shrugged, "I guess they're just not for me."

"Probably understandable," Sand said, returning with two beers. He handed one to Stone.

"I never thought of that before, but yeah, I guess I associate… bad vibes with the hunt. I don't want to meet a female like that." The hunt had left a bad taste in his mouth.

"How then?" Macy asked. "It's not like there are many opportunities available."

"I don't know." Stone shook his head. "I'm not worried. It will happen one day. It'll happen in a way that it is meant to. I'm sure we'll take one look at each other and we'll just know. It'll be love at first sight."

Sand choked out a laughed. "Yeah right!"

Macy chuckled as well. It was good to see her a little more light-hearted.

"It never happens that way, bro." Sand shook his head.

What was complicated about it? Love was straightforward. He'd know. He'd act and that would be that.

CHAPTER 2

Six weeks later…

The human clutched her glass so tightly her knuckles turned white. She took a small sip that was more for show than to quench her thirst. There was something worrying her friend. That much was evident. Cordia wanted to ask her what that something was. Instead, she held her tongue. The human would tell her when she was good and ready.

"So, when do you leave for the conference?" Vicky asked; she smiled but it was tight.

"Tomorrow." Cordia took a sip of her own juice.

"Are you excited?"

"Of course." She licked her lips. "However. I need to keep my expectations low. There is no cure for our species' affliction, or for—"

"You don't know that." Vicky leaned forward, putting

her glass down on the table.

They'd had this conversation several times before. The human was forever the optimist. Vicky hadn't seen the death. She hadn't lost friends and family. Cordia's chest tightened as she thought of her sister. Each and every fertile female of their species fell ill and died in the space of just over two years. It was devastating. "We need to look at finding a cure for clutch sickness, as well as cures for the infertile females of the other species."

Vicky frowned. "It's more than finding a cure. There may not be one for every species affected. Talon mentioned it's to find solutions to the problems surrounding infertility, rather than a cure. Although, a cure would be first prize." Her ever-positive friend did not believe that humans would be affected by the disease that had ravaged so many of their kind.

Cordia was not so certain. "We do need to find a cure for clutch sickness as it could affect you humans as well. I must say, I'm looking forward to this conference but at the same time..." Cordia sighed. "I'm not all that hopeful." Her heart did beat faster at the prospect of a solution. It wasn't going to be long before the first human mated to a Feral decided to try for a clutch. What then? Would they be affected too? Would they die?

"You don't look like you're looking forward to it." Vicky looked at her with concern.

"It's a small-scale conference. More to explore topics and options for future meetings." Cordia sighed. "What kind of solution could there possibly be for us?" Cordia didn't see it. "Non-human males are not interested in infertile females and human males are easily broken. Our males might like soft, simpering human females and may be attracted to vulnerable beings needing protecting. It doesn't work the other way around though." She shuddered at the mere thought of a puny human male. Even the other species seemed puny to her. Her own males shunned her most of the time, which suited her perfectly.

Vicky choked out a laugh. "*I* am one of those weak, simpering humans, you know?"

Cordia smiled. "You know what I mean. It wasn't a slight against you. You're my best friend."

Vicky's gaze softened. She leaned forward and squeezed Cordia's hand. "You're my best friend as well." She chewed on her lower lip, her eyes turning… sad and then panicky. She picked up her glass, white knuckles evident again, and drank. This time she took a big swig of the juice, half choking.

"You okay?" Cordia asked.

"Yes." Vicky smiled, pulling in a deep breath, her eyes shone from coughing.

"Are you going to tell me what's going on?" Cordia asked.

That panicky look was back. "There is nothing going on. Everything is…" Her shoulders slumped. "We don't want to wait anymore." She put her glass down with a thud.

Cordia felt an icy fist grip her heart, knowing immediately what Vicky was referring to.

"We've been together for almost a year now and…" She bit down on her lip for a second. "We're going to try for a clutch. We want—"

Cordia stood up. "No!" Even though the word was whispered, it was filled with such emotion that Vicky blanched.

"I'm not a Feral." Vicky shook her head. "I'm sure it will be fine. It *will* be fine."

"Why you? Why not one of the others?"

"Kerry and Cadon have their child." A human child who Cadon had adopted as his own. "The others are newly mated. It—"

"Wait!" Cordia begged, her heart clenching so hard she felt physical pain inside her chest. "You need to have just a little more patience. It will only be a matter of time before—"

"We don't want to wait anymore. We love each other. We want children. Someone has to be first. I will be the one." She sucked in a deep breath.

Cordia sat down, heavily. The sofa creaked. She leaned back feeling drained. "And Talon is okay with this?" Adrenaline coursed through her veins. How did she stop this? "He can't be okay with it." The male had lost his mate to the ghastly sickness.

Vicky shrugged. "No. He is worried. He hasn't slept much since we decided a few days ago that we were going to go for it."

"You could get the sickness. You would die if you did. It is a horrific death." She could still scent it. Still taste death on her tongue. There in the room even before it claimed its victims. She could still hear her sister's agonized moans. She shut her eyes for a moment trying to block the images and sounds that accosted her. The memories that sometimes threatened to overwhelm her. "You can't!" She gripped Vicky's hand and squeezed, before letting go.

Vicky swallowed thickly. "I'm not a Feral female. I'm a

human. Chances are good I'll be fine."

"But you don't know that for sure." Cordia shook her head.

"No."

"It's too big a risk then." She tried to keep the emotion from her voice and failed.

Vicky touched Cordia on the side of the arm, leaving her hand there. "It's worth it. I don't know how you do it. How you—"

"This conversation is not about me. I'm worried!" Cordia swallowed thickly.

"I know." Vicky nodded. "Dying would be worst-case scenario and I can't see it coming to that."

None of them had seen clutch sickness coming. That was the problem. Yet it had come, and it had taken many lives.

Her friend's voice was high-pitched. "Can you at least try to be happy for us?" She raised her brows, her eyes filled with expectation. They were also brimming with tears.

Cordia felt her shoulders slump. "I am worried that's all. Of course, I am," she grit her teeth for a moment, "happy for you and Talon. I wish you all of the very best." She nodded. "I wish you would reconsider though."

"We've made up our minds."

Cordia suppressed a sigh. She forced her mouth to tilt into something she hoped looked like a smile. "Then I am happy for you and I support you both." Her heart felt heavy.

Vicky smiled. "Thank you!"

Cordia nodded, still trying to smile. Trying to push the cloying fear aside. Surely the gods wouldn't be so cruel as to take Vicky from her as well. Talon had also suffered terribly. Surely, he wouldn't be made to suffer the loss of another mate to clutch sickness. It couldn't happen!

CHAPTER 3

Cordia was eager for the events of the day to begin. She was eager to find more than just a solution to their problems. She wanted a cure. Had to find one. This wasn't about her anymore. It wasn't even about her fellow Feral females who were afflicted with infertility issues. It was about Vicky. Her best friend, who even then might be going into her heat. Who even then might be signing her own death warrant. *May the gods protect her!*

There were two open seats across from her. Annoyance rose up but she forced it down. The conference was due to begin in four and a half minutes. Where were these delegates? Why weren't they there yet? Did they not take this whole discussion seriously? It might be a precursor to future events, but it was important. She forced her annoyance down. There was still time. They weren't late yet.

She looked to her left. All of the chairs were filled with

females from all of the species. Cordia could not wait to hear from them. To learn from them. This was—

That's when they walked in. The dragons. *What?* She felt her brow crease. *What was a male doing there? Was it a joke perhaps?* A bad joke for sure.

Just like others from her species, she didn't have the best sense of smell. She could still pick up hints of smokiness coming off them. She had referred to all males from the other species as being puny.

Puny and weak.

This male was anything but. He instantly seemed to fill the room. He instantly drew the eye of every female in attendance. Was it her imagination or did it turn quiet for a good couple of beats?

No. It wasn't. They all stared. They all looked. They all took notice, sizing him up.

The male was tall and hard as rock. His muscles rippled beneath his skin. His eyes were... they were quite beautiful. The color of jewels. His mouth...

By feather! What was she doing? What was this male doing there? An imposter. Anger rose up in her. Firstly, at herself for being attracted to this... to him and then even more anger at herself for allowing the emotion to take her in the first place.

The dragon looked around the table and then sat down. He instantly locked eyes with her as he did. Even more good-looking up close. *Bastard male!* He had no right to be there. *None!*

Cordia narrowed her eyes at him, giving him what she hoped was a scathing look. Waiting for him to look away. The male didn't, he kept his eyes on hers for a good long while. Long enough to have something take up residence in the pit of her stomach.

She wanted that something gone. It irritated her. He irritated her. Just when she thought it couldn't get worse, his eyes moved down to her chest. That thing in the pit of her stomach tightened. There was a tug on her clit as his eyes brushed her chest. Almost like she could feel his gaze physically.

His nostrils flared and she imagined she saw something in his gaze… need… hunger. Of course she did. All males were the same. They all wanted a tight snatch. *Bastards!*

"Um…" He turned his body slightly to the dragon female next to him. The male didn't take his eyes off of her though. She made sure to match that stare. Gaze unwavering. Cordia grit her teeth, frowning. "I thought the brief said a male and a female from each species. Why am I the only male in attendance?"

She couldn't help the snort that was ripped from her. Who did he think he was? *What an idiot!* "The brief *recommended* that a male and a female attend." Why was she having to explain this? The Feral were considered the least educated of all the species. It was something they were working on. "The word 'recommended' is key here. Who would send a male? What would a male know about issues concerning female fertility? You should not be here." She wanted to take him by the hair and yank him from the room. She wanted to hurt him… just a little. That feeling inside returned. The tightening. She wanted to… *No!*

The male didn't flinch. Cordia felt a begrudging respect for a few moments until she remembered where they were. Who he was. Why they were there. The female next to him leaned forward, eyes on Cordia. "Our king was the one who made the call." She glanced at the male. "Stone

---

was ordered to attend, as was I. The male is eager to contribute to our discussions surrounding—"

"Then your king is a fool," she spat, unable to hold back. *A male? What did a male know?* How could a male ever understand or contribute? He was a waste of air. Cordia, all of them there, needed individuals who could actually weigh in. It was imperative if they were going to find a cure.

"Do not—" the female dragon began, venom shining in her eyes.

The male dragon touched her arm, preventing her from saying anything more. "I am already here," he kept his voice even; it was deep and resonating, "so, I would appreciate it if we could make the most of it. I assure you I will take my role as delegate very seriously."

Cordia snorted again. She was expected to buy that nonsense? "We are here to discuss the predicament of infertile, non-human females. You are neither of those. In fact, why aren't you with a human right now? Making young? You have absolutely no idea what it is like to—"

"Come now, Cordia," Surora said, touching the side of her arm for a second. "The dragon sounds like he has genuine concern for our plight. He has been tasked with attending, as have we. Let's not—"

"I don't like it." Cordia pushed her dark hair back off her shoulder. Not one bit. His presence would only serve as a distraction. There was no way in hell he would be able to contribute. Surely the others could see that? "Maybe we should take a vote. Your king can send a female in your place when everyone votes for you to leave. Someone sympathetic to what we are going through. That person is not you, male." She widened her eyes. All of the females there were suffering from this predicament. He clearly was not.

"Stop right there!" the female dragon blurted. "You have no idea—"

"Leave it," the male interrupted. "It's not worth it," he added. For a moment his eyes seemed to flash with something. It made her want to leave it alone. Then that look was gone, and those beautiful piercing eyes seemed to look right into her.

"You said we should vote," a female from down the other end of the table drew their attention. "I vote that the dragon stays." She smiled at the male, giving him a wink.

Cordia held back an eyeroll but only just.

"I agree," the wolf shifter sitting next to her said, licking her lips. "Let him stay. The rest of us are all infertile females. One male will help us see things from another angle. He would bring something... new to the table."

Right! This time, there was no way to hold back the eyeroll. She grit her teeth for a moment, trying to find some calm. "You are only saying that because the male is attractive. He has pretty eyes and a decent-sized prick. You're hoping for a rut and want to get on his good side. I saw the way all of you looked at him when he came into the room. This is serious." Her voice boomed. How did she make them see? Why weren't they taking this seriously? There were females counting on them.

"You looked at my dick when I entered the room?" The male's lip twitched.

What a horse's ass! "Not on purpose. Your midsection is at exactly eye level. I was already sitting here when you came in. You are wearing those thin cotton pants." She shrugged, pointing out the facts as she saw them. "It was hard to miss. I assure you, I wasn't looking." She snorted. *As if! Idiot male. So arrogant! So infuriating!*

The dragon female giggled.

Just then, another female walked in. She wore a navy dress suit with a white blouse. She was holding a glass bowl with folded pieces of paper inside. "Morning!" She smiled warmly at all of them.

Cordia held her breath, waiting to see if she addressed the dragon male. She waited for her to ask him why he was there.

It didn't happen. "I am Gazelle," she went on. "Welcome to vampire territory. I have been tasked with coordinating our conference over the next few days. We have a couple of interesting topics up for discussion. I thought it would be a good idea if the species were split up. I want each of us out of our comfort zones and learning about one another, while we figure out a way forward for all females," she cleared her throat, "like ourselves."

Not him!

Cordia couldn't help but to glare at the dragon. He glanced her way, holding her gaze for a good few moments. She hated that her cheeks heated.

Thankfully, he finally looked away and she was able to breathe.

"Here," Gazelle put the glass bowl on the table, "I want each of you on this side of the table to take one piece of folded up paper. Do not open it yet!" The bowl began making its way down to the dragons. Each one on the opposite side of the table removed a slip. The male did too, placing the empty bowl on the table in front of him.

He held onto the paper.

Let it be anyone but him, Cordia willed. *Anyone but him!*

"On three, you can open up and see who your partner will be for the duration of the conference. You will work closely with this person. I am sure that together, we can find a way forward, or at least make a start on how to begin to tackle this very serious issue. You may open your papers now and then we will take a one-hour recess so that you can get to know your partner better." She smiled broadly, sucking in a deep breath before counting down. "One, two… three. You may open the paper now."

The male looked at the scrap in his hand for a few seconds longer than the rest before finally opening it. Cordia knew instantly that her name was written down on it. She could tell by the way his jaw tightened. By the way he shifted in his seat. By the way he now avoided her gaze.

By feather and tar! This was a farce!

"Go and enjoy some light refreshments," the female addressed them. "Make sure you go somewhere private with your partner. I want you to fully understand one another, as a species, by the time this conference is over. We will discuss each species and fertility problems pertaining to each one. I want us to fully understand where similarities lie but also issues that are unique to a particular species. I'm sure we can learn enormous amounts from one another."

"Why the need for the whole team-building thing?" the dragon asked, looking agitated. At least he hated the idea of pairing with her as much as she did. She should be happy with the idea, but it left her feeling… she wasn't sure. By now she was used to being ignored by males of her own kind. Ignored. Set aside and shunned. Why would this dragon make her feel any different? Besides, she had started this feud first. It shouldn't bug her, but it did. That, in turn, irritated her all over again. *Blasted dragon!*

"We all share a common problem," Gazelle said. "However, it is far more complex than that and aspects may differ between the species. Who knows? Maybe one species can help another. Knowledge is always power. We will never know unless we share. Our kings would also like for this to be an opportunity where we improve our interspecies relationships. Take it as a chance to learn and to grow. Your hour has started." She looked at the watch on her wrist.

There was loud chatter and chairs scraped as new pairs began to leave. Everyone eventually upped and left, including Gazelle. Eventually, it was only the two of them remaining. Still sitting there across from one another. "I do not wish to improve interspecies relationships. Not with you at any rate." Cordia shook her head, needing to get this across to him. "I don't like you." It needed to be said.

He frowned. "How do you even know that? You don't know me."

"You're a non-human and a male. Both reasons enough."

"Bullshit," the male countered. "Those are the worst reasons I have ever heard. Very general and quite biased."

Cordia raised her brows. "Dragon, vampire, Feral, shifter or elf. You males are all the same." All out to get one thing and one thing only. A good mounting and then young. Not being able to get the latter didn't deter them from going after the aforementioned.

"What?" he snorted. "I've never heard such shit in all my life."

"You looked at my breasts… sized me up when you first arrived. You pictured rutting me at least once in the short time we have been in the same room. In short, you reduced me to an object before you knew anything about me. If I offered to rut you right now, you would jump at the opportunity."

"Are you offering?" He folded his hands on the table, leaning forward slightly, looking like he was serious.

That tightening in her belly returned. For a moment she was tempted to acknowledge the offer, just to see what would happen. Instead, she rolled her eyes, before narrowing them on him. "You wouldn't last even one round." *Puny dragon.* "I would hurt you."

He snorted again. "Like hell you would."

"Then again," she raised her brows, "if you were hurt, you would need to return to your lair, tail between your legs and I wouldn't have to look at you anymore. I quite like that idea." She pretended to consider the notion, which she wasn't seriously doing of course.

He laughed, actually sounding nervous. *Good!* He needed to be afraid.

She leaned forward, placing her hands on the table as well. "You're afraid." She smiled. "I can tell… and so you should be. Walk away now before you are injured… or worse."

"The only thing that would get injured are your vocal cords – from all the screaming when I make you come."

She felt a zing deep in the pit of her stomach. It seemed to reach out and tug on her nipples and her clit. Cordia pulled in a sharp intake of air and stood up to stop the feeling of need that accosted her. It had been years since she had been with a male. So long she had forgotten what it felt like. "That would be most difficult if you were broken and possibly even bleeding. You'd turn me on. Get me going and then have to leave to see a healer. It would happen before the grand finale. In short, you'd leave me hanging. Not interested, dragon!" she snorted.

"Hanging? Huh! Like hell!" He stood up as well. His muscles bulged. His prick… by feather and by scale… his prick was hard. She could see its long, thick shape easily through the thin coverings he was wearing. It was even more impressive than she had first realized. She forced her eyes back up to his narrowed stare. The male licked his lips. "The only way I'll leave you is with a dripping wet pussy from an orgasm that will rock you to your core. I'll leave you sweating, panting and wanting a whole lot more." The male was so confident it bordered on arrogance. Perversely, she liked that about him.

Cordia glanced down at her chest before looking up at him, realizing that she was breathing heavily. She was holding onto the edge of the table with such force that she heard a soft cracking noise. She forced herself to let go.

His nostrils were flared. His eyes bright and feverish.

"You'd break… puny dragon. My hold would fracture you. My snatch would break your prick in two." Her voice was a mere whisper. "Is that something you desire?"

"You could," he smirked, "try to break me." He bit down on his lower lip for a second. "I must say, I might enjoy being broken by you Feral." His eyes drifted back down to her chest. She knew he would see how hard her nipples were. His nostrils flared again. Cordia knew he would scent how wet she had become.

"I would have to try *not* to break you. Therein lies the problem," she countered. They should stop this madness.

"I doubt I could manage it."

"Come here and let's find out." He motioned to her with two fingers.

"If you want pain so badly, *you* come here and get it."

Using one arm, the dragon propelled himself easily across the table, landing silently next to her. The male pulled himself to his full height. Her eyes went up and up. Just as she suspected, he was taller than her by a couple of inches. Outweighed her too.

The dragon leaned in, not quite touching her. He sniffed at her.

That tightening came back at the pit of her stomach. Tighter, tighter, coiling, coiling, pulling...

"Interesting. You don't have a scent," he growled the words while sniffing her skin again. Gooseflesh rose up on her arms, especially where he almost made contact with her. Then the one side of his mouth lifted. "Your pussy smells good though. Fucking delicious."

Her heart thrummed with excitement. She shouldn't be doing this. As a dragon, the male had an excellent sense of smell. Fantastic senses.

There was risk involved in doing this. Major risk. She wasn't joking about hurting him. There were so many reasons why she shouldn't. Her friend... Vicky. Finding solutions to the many problems. The weight seemed unbearable at this moment. The years of loneliness suddenly felt unbearable too. This was completely wrong. She needed to walk away right now.

The dragon licked his lips, his eyes on her mouth. His gaze filled with desire... for her. It had been a long time since a male had looked at her like that. Cordia decided to throw caution to the wind. This one time and one time only. She smiled at him as she took his prick in a solid grip.

The dragon grunted. She tightened her fingers just a smidgen more and he made a noise in the back of his throat. The muscles on either side of his neck corded as he grit his teeth. "Are you sure you want to do this? Think very carefully before answering." She had expected his prick to go soft in her hands. Instead, it throbbed and seemed to grow.

It looked like he might surprise her yet.

CHAPTER 4

Her hold was so tight it hurt him – he was obviously a sick fuck because it also felt damned good. His balls tightened with need. Those piercing yellow eyes seemed to see right into him. They were calm, calculating and yet… gorgeous. Like thick, sweet honey, or the rising sun on a clear winter's morning. Her lashes were long. Her pupils wide and contrasting. The female herself was too tall and too toned to be deemed beautiful, but fuck was she sexy. From her long dark tresses to her ripe little tits that were trying to free themselves from the tight confines of her shirt. Everything about her screamed of raw energy, of raw power. She also scared the hell out of him. Fortunately, or maybe unfortunately, all of it turned him on.

"I want to do this," he said and then grunted as she let him go. Stone wasn't sure if it was relief or frustration that caused the sound to be pulled from his body.

"You're going to be sorry." She pushed at his chest using one hand.

Stone had to put a hand back onto the cold wood of the table to stop himself from stumbling back, from falling on his ass... which he nearly did. She was even stronger than she looked. Sexy as sin. It seemed she wanted him on his back. That, or she wanted to run the show. He shook his head. "That's not how this is going down."

"It would be safest for you if—"

"Fuck being safe! I have superior healing abilities." He shook his head again. "I'm not afraid of you, Feral."

"You should be, dragon."

"I'm not!" He put his hands on her hips and picked her up. Only just managing to get her off of the ground and nearly pulling several muscles in his back. The Feral was heavy. Stone quickly thought better of that. He put her back down as her full mouth curled into a knowing smile. "See, I told you I—" She groaned, her eyes drifting shut as his thumb found her clit. It was easy since her skirt was badass short, and since she wasn't wearing any underwear. He zoned in on that tight bundle of nerves, dipping down briefly to coat his finger in her juices before moving back. Her mouth opened slightly, her head falling back a little as her grip on his arms tightened. She made little breathless noises. Stone kept up his assault, his finger slipping and sliding in easy circles that had her moaning again. Her breathing was choppy, her grip becoming painful on his arms.

"Lie down," he commanded, wanting to feast on her.

"No." She let him go, sounding a little frazzled. "Let's do this. Take me from behind." Her voice was laced with need. Her eyes were glassy. The female leaned over the table, yanking up her skirt around her hips. "I'm ready for you."

Her ass was tight. Her pussy was flushed a gorgeous dark pink. It glistened with her juices. Definitely ripe for the taking. He knew it wouldn't take much. A minute or two at the most. She could keep her hands on the table. He'd be safe as houses. They could both get off and walk away unscathed. Then maybe they'd be able to get back to the business at hand. The reason they were there. This strange attraction, this madness could end.

Stone had never taken the easy road before and he wouldn't start now. He turned her around to face him. Her cheeks were flushed. Her lips were plump. Maybe she was beautiful after all. "Open your legs," he growled.

"You like giving orders?" She narrowed her eyes on his.

"Do it!" he insisted, going down onto his knees.

Thankfully, she complied. Stone bunched her skirt up with one hand and found her clit with his mouth. Fuck but she tasted good. He used his tongue to lave her, using quick strokes. She moaned and fisted his hair, quickly letting go. Thank claw! Any harder and he would have lost a chunk.

He was being an idiot by doing this, but he didn't care. He changed direction, laving her clit in tight circles. Her pants and moans were becoming louder. Not long now. He closed his mouth over her and suckled, really going to town, suckling her clit like his life depended on it.

She gave a shriek. It was high-pitched and lasted all of a second before she clamped her mouth shut. Unfortunately, she clamped her legs shut around him as well. He heard something crack. Felt pain like a livewire inside his torso.

Thank fuck he was a dragon and used to dealing with a significant amount of pain. The males sparred and regularly hurt one another. Broken limbs were not uncommon. He gave her clit one last suck as she was coming down, then stood. He held back a grunt as pain flared back up. *Holy fuck, she hadn't been kidding.*

At least his legs still worked. *Great!* There was quite a bit of pain on one side of his torso, but he could deal with it. The pain in his cock and balls was much greater. The need to be inside her far more urgent than regrouping and checking for injury. Besides, there was no way he was giving her the satisfaction of seeing him hurt. She had said she would break him and break him she had. Even before his cock came anywhere near her pussy. He'd take it as a compliment though.

The Feral was breathing heavily. Her eyes at half-mast. She was clutching a chunk of torn off table in one hand. Thank fuck she hadn't been holding onto him or he might be bleeding out around about now. One of his limbs in her hand. It would have been worth it though and regeneration was a thing. The female had enjoyed his attentions. By the juices running down her inner thighs, she had enjoyed it very much.

"I want you," he pushed out.

She nodded, still breathing heavily. She dropped the chunk of wood, which clattered on the ground.

Stone clasped her hip and turned her around, yanking his pants down with the other hand. He felt frantic with need.

The Feral pushed out her ass in a silent invitation. One he took. Stone took her hips and plunged into her, bottoming out on the first thrust. He snarled and she yelled. "So fucking wet," he ground out as he pulled back. He thrust into her again, and again, and again. Loving the greedy sucking sounds her body made. The table made a creaking noise but held. His eyes squeezed shut on the next thrust. "Holy fuck but you feel good," he growled.

Tight.

Wet.

Hot.

By the sounds she was making he could tell she was enjoying it too. The table scraped against the floor every few thrusts. In short, they were noisy. Part of him wondered if maybe they should try to keep quiet. Where were the other delegates? What would they be thinking right then if they were listening in?

Her pussy tightened around him and Stone found that he no longer cared. Couldn't remember where they were, or even his own damned name for that matter. The entire delegation could walk in and he wouldn't stop. His balls were tight. Pulling up high. Almost in his throat. Her hands were flat on the table. Her body too, her ass high in the air. *Lovely.* There was more tightening around his dick, her velvet channel seemed to hold onto him, pulling him deeper.

Stone gripped her hips tighter and groaned, trying hard to keep from coming like a teenager. He wanted to. Needed it almost more than he needed his next breath. His balls slapped against her ass as he ground into her. He didn't have to be careful, or gentle. The Feral could take his cock. *All of it.* It felt amazing. His legs shook with the need to come. His whole body vibrated with it. She moaned and made strange other species noises that told him she was close. *Not close enough! Not nearly!*

Stone shoved his hand between her and the table. She was leaning down, her chest almost flush against the wood. Her eyes were closed. Her mouth open. He strummed on her clit like a man possessed, continuing his assault on her pussy, using deep, hard thrusts.

Her body visibly tightened as her pussy pulsed and fluttered around him. She made an ear-piercing screeching noise as her back bowed. Then it happened.

Stone sucked in a deep breath, the air seizing in his lungs. His eyes widened. Sweat beaded on his brow. His mouth sagged open. He'd never felt anything like it. He doubted he ever would ever again.

Her pussy… it… it—He roared as his balls emptied in one quick, shocking ejaculation that took his breath away all over again. It was like he was being punched in the gut but instead of pain, sheer pleasure hit him. The inside of her channel had closed even tighter around him where his tip was inside her. The deepest section. *Fuck! Fuck!* He groaned deep; it felt like a few scales might have popped out on his chest. He struggled to breathe as more seed was pulled from him. Like he was being milked. Her pussy seemed to be suctioning the end of his dick. Like he was fucking and getting head at the same time. It was like nothing he had ever felt before. He finally pulled in a breath and then roared all over again. Long, hard and deep. His body jerked, practically convulsing from the sheer pleasure that still rolled through him. Eventually, the sensations ebbed. He slowed his movements, finally collapsing over her. He felt spent. Like every limb had been stripped of energy.

The Feral was panting. She giggled. It was a melodic sound. Strange coming from one so fierce and strong. He finally managed to lift his head. "What?" he croaked.

"We might be in trouble." She giggled again; her back vibrated against his chest.

Stone cussed. He hadn't even noticed the table collapsing. How the hell hadn't he noticed such a thing? They were on the wooden surface, on the floor. The stack of papers that had been on the far side of the table were scattered on the floor. The table legs were a shattered, splintered mess.

The rutting had been that good, that's how he hadn't noticed. Even now, her pussy still suctioned him. He wondered if there would be a popping sound if he withdrew. Something told him not to try just yet. It might hurt. Besides, Stone enjoyed being inside her. They still had – he glanced at the clock – almost half an hour. Maybe they should get to know each other some more.

Stone chuckled. "I guess everyone will know what we've been up to." He noticed how her smile lit up her whole face. She was definitely far more attractive than he had first given her credit for.

"You made enough noi—" the Feral began.

The door to the conference room opened and the vampire female walked in. Her eyes widened and she burst out laughing as she caught sight of them.

Stone crouched over the Feral, his chest to her back. On his knees. His cock was still deep inside the female, his hand wrapped around her middle. He didn't make a move to pull out.

One of the wolf shifters was next in; her eyes widened as they landed on them. She broke out into peals of laughter. Topaz poked her head around the jamb. She scrunched her eyes shut and made a noise of exasperation.

"Really?" Topaz put a hand over her face, mostly covering her eyes.

Then the vampire Gazelle walked in. Her eyes widened and she shrieked before quickly exiting the room.

The Feral didn't move an inch either. She had pulled herself up onto her elbows. She held the gazes of the females at the door, not looking in the least perturbed. She didn't try to cover up, or to explain.

Topaz rolled her eyes and left with a sigh. The other two followed, more slowly.

"They said to get to know each other!" Stone shouted after their retreating backs. The door clinked shut.

He eased out of her, grunting as he did so. "Holy fuck!" he muttered to himself. "We probably should have used a condom." More loudly this time. "I can't believe I forgot. Then again," he gave his head a shake, "you are infertile, aren't you?"

She turned over, her eyes narrowing into his. "I have heard of these coverings. They are made from a stretchy substance called…" She lifted her eyes. "I can't remember…"

"Rubber. They're made from rubber."

She nodded once. "That's it. They are made for humans." She shrugged. "They more than likely won't work anyway."

"They may be made for humans, but they *do* work… mostly. It is very rare that there is a mishap." He sniffed the air. "You don't scent like you're going into heat or anything." He didn't want to be rude, or push her. He didn't want to make her feel uncomfortable bringing something up that was most likely a sore point for her, but he had to know. It was important. "You are… infertile…

I mean, surely you wouldn't be here otherwise?" He felt himself frown. Felt the frown deepen with each passing second. How the fuck had this happened? How had he gotten so carried away?

"So, I was right?" She narrowed her eyes, her jaw tightening. "You are able to have young. Why are you here, dragon?" Immediately on the defense. Before he could say anything, she went on. The Feral nodded once. "To answer your question, I am at an infertility conference after all."

"Yes, you are." He pulled up his pants, noting that she made no attempt to cover herself.

"I'm Stone," he held out his hand, "by the way."

She sat up, finally pulling her skirt down, ignoring his gesture flat. It didn't look like she was going to reciprocate by telling him her name.

Stone lowered his hand. "I know your colleague said your name earlier, but… I'm sorry, I can't remember what it is."

"Just because you mounted me does not mean that we are friends now." She shook her head. "Nothing has changed. I still want you gone." She shrugged matter-of-factly.

"Unfortunately, you're stuck with me," he replied. "We're partners."

"You can call me Feral. I will keep calling you dragon." She stood up. "I really wish you would reconsider leaving. You have no right to be here."

"You're wrong, Feral." He stood up as well, trying hard not to wince, or to show any outward signs of discomfort. He would wager that at least two of his ribs were cracked. "We will have to agree to disagree on that one."

Her jaw tensed and her gorgeous eyes narrowed in irritation. "I am glad you survived the mounting. That you were able to bring me to completion. You are stronger than I thought." She pushed out what sounded like a bored sigh. *Surely not!* Their coming together had been anything but boring. "But that won't be happening again."

"Yet again, we're going to have to agree to disagree."

"It won't!" She shook her head. "You can forget it."

"It will and you can bet on it."

"Look, we needed to get that out of the way. It happened and now it's done. The itch has been lanced."

Stone bit down on his lip to keep from laughing. "Don't you mean scratched?"

She frowned. "What?"

"The itch has been scratched. That's the right way of saying it."

She shrugged, deadpan. "Whatever! Scratched, lanced... same thing. It's done. It's out of the way. Now you should leave, so that the females can get down to work."

"Not happening... *and* I look forward to more itch-scratching."

The Feral shook her head and made a sound of frustration as she began picking up the scattered papers. Storm followed suit. He couldn't help the grin that spread across his face. What an unexpected turn of events.

CHAPTER 5

"I can't believe you." Topaz shook her head. She looked pissed off. Her eyes blazed.

"It's not a big deal." Stone shrugged.

"You broke the table. Everyone knows you rutted that Feral. Helga and Lexi saw the two of you… you were still… you…" She made a face. "It can't be unseen." She rubbed her eyes like she was trying to do just that.

"It wasn't such a big deal," Stone tried again. "We were told to get to know each other better."

Topaz gave him a dirty look. "Don't even go there." She widened her eyes. "I have never heard a male make so much noise… ever. I couldn't believe what I was hearing. She really did a number on you. Are you sure it's just your ribs she broke?" She glanced at where he was clutching his chest.

The Feral had done a number on him alright. Only, it hadn't hurt. Not in the least. Maybe just then in the aftermath – just a little – but it had all been worth it. He couldn't wait to do it again. As far as he was concerned, she could break more bones, even tear off a limb… as long as it was that particular appendage.

More.

He wanted more.

"Get that grin off your face." Topaz punched him on the arm. "This is serious. I thought you of all people would take this conference seriously. The first thing you do is rut the person you've been paired with."

Her words had him sobering in an instant. "I *do* take it seriously. Very seriously. There was no way that Feral wanted anything to do with me." *She still didn't.* "I was trying to turn that around so that we could work together and make progress." It was mostly true. At least, that's how it had started out. He hadn't meant to take it that far. It just happened. Arguing one second and fucking the next. It was addictive.

"You tried to get her onto your side using your cock. How did that work out for you?" She folded her arms.

"Not all that well," he admitted. "She hates me even more now."

Topaz snorted. "She doesn't hate you. That didn't look like a female who hates you. Her name is Cordia, by the way."

He smiled and nodded vigorously. "Oh yes!" He cleared his throat feeling like an asshole. "Thanks."

"If you want to get on her good side, best you remember her name and best you get serious about this conference." She pointed at him, wagging her finger. Deservedly of course.

"I *am* serious! Fuck!" He grit his teeth for a moment.

"How could I not be?" Stone swallowed thickly. "After everything… after…" He looked down at the floor, clenching his jaw.

Topaz put an arm around him. "I know you are. You just have to *show* that you are."

He nodded. "You're right."

"No more messing with the Feral." She widened her eyes.

"I kind of liked messing with her, but I won't do it during conference hours. I won't break any more tables either."

"You need to stay away from her, Stone. They are too different. The kings will have your balls if they find out what happened today."

"The kings said to use this as an opportunity to improve interspecies relationships. That's what I did. I plan on working really hard on improving our relationship with the Ferals. Starting with a certain Feral named Cordia."

Topaz laughed. "You are full of it. That's not what they meant, and you know it."

He smiled. "I swear, I take this seriously and I will make it my aim to prove it with nothing but exemplary behavior. What I do outside of working hours is my business." He raised his brows.

Topaz nodded. "Okay then." She shrugged. "I guess I can't disagree with that."

The vampire smiled, exposing long, ivory fangs. They were sharp looking. It was weird Gazelle didn't have them. Cordia was sure that when she'd seen this female earlier that morning when they'd first arrived here, her teeth had looked normal as well. Yet there they were, gleaming and sharp. Just as sharp as the female's smile, which she kept on flashing at him… the blasted dragon.

The male sat there, leaning back in his chair like he didn't have a care in the world.

Eyes forward!

Cordia didn't want him to think she was interested in him. Just because she'd let him mount her one measly time. Problem was, she wanted to look at him so badly. To keep tabs, of course. To make sure he was paying attention.

The dragon hadn't broken like she thought he would. He wasn't puny or inept. He'd been good. Better than just plain good. Her body still vibrated. Endorphins still flooded her system. They didn't make her feel good though. They made her want more. Made her feel edgy and needy. She'd forgotten how much she craved physical contact. It was normal for her to feel this way.

The vamp flashed the arrogant male another sexy smile, lowering her lashes. Cordia forced herself to pay attention to what she was saying.

"There are two kinds of fertility problems that vampires are facing," she went on, looking around the room. "Some of our females can't have children. They do not go into heat. Others, like me…" She smiled at Cordia; it had a sly edge. Maybe it was just her imagination. "… are fertile, very much so." The sly, sexy smile was back and directed at the dragon. "That doesn't mean that we are capable of birthing vampire young. You see our hips are too narrow. Vampire young are large. We are pregnant for almost a year. Longer than a human female. The infant cannot pass through our pelvis." She ran her hands down her hips, which were, indeed, very narrow. "There are very few vampire females capable of birthing our own young, hence why the program was started and human females introduced to mate with our elite males." She pushed out a breath, taking a sip of her water. "It's been effective and many babies have been born, all with vampire traits."

"A program was supposed to be introduced for fertile vampire females with narrow hips as well. You see," more fluttering of the lashes at the male – it was glaringly obvious that this female was interested in him, "we can breed successfully with shifters." She winked at the dragon.

Winked!

By feather and tar. Cordia rolled her eyes. Did she have no respect for herself? This was the vampire who had walked in on them having sex a few hours before.

"Shifter pregnancies are shorter, only six months. Am I right, Stone? Is it the same with dragons as well?" She giggled, fangs flashing.

"Yes… for most of our kind." He nodded once. "I'm an Earth dragon and it is true for us."

"Good to know." Another wink.

Blast and damn but she was laying it on thick. Cordia cleared her throat and tried to get more comfortable. Her chair was hard. Maybe they should leave the two lovebirds alone?

"We are nearly out of time, Helga," Gazelle said looking at her watch, "can you wrap up for us, please? We'll continue tomorrow."

The vampire nodded, smiling sweetly. "I'm excited for this new program to be introduced. We were told it would be, but that was over a year ago already. It would be nice if things could move along. The program for the males seemed to have happened overnight. We haven't been as lucky. There is talk but no action."

"Why not spearhead it yourself?" Cordia asked.

The vampire looked at her like she was a bug that had just crawled out from under a rock. "My kings will ensure that our program is launched… at some point," she added with a pained expression.

"You just expressed concern at how long it is taking. Have you enquired as to the progress?" she tried again.

The vampire shook her head. "I have plenty of patience. I'm sure something will give." Another wink at the dragon.

By claw, but this female was too much. Cordia bit down on her tongue to prevent herself from saying something she might regret. Something that could get her sent home. This conference was important. She had slipped up with the male. Had taken risks that could land her in hot water. She needed to watch her step.

"Okay," Gazelle stepped forward, "thank you for sharing. Dinner is at six. We've made it a little earlier tonight as I'm sure you're all tired after an early start this morning. It's been a taxing day." She pressed her lips together looking amused as she glanced at Cordia and Stone. Her cheeks turned red.

Cordia felt her own cheeks heat. "Would it be okay if I ordered in, instead of meeting in the dining room?" Cordia asked. She was tired. Exhausted.

"Um… we had thought that you could share meals together, as a way of bonding," Gazelle looked unsure, "but I suppose…"

"Thank you," Cordia said before the female could change her mind.

Gazelle spoke some more about their agenda for the following day, being very cryptic about what was happening during the course of the morning. She finally told them they were done. Cordia sprang off of her seat like it was on fire. She raced from the room, taking three steps in the direction of her nest when a sultry voice piped up behind her. "Where are you running off to, partner?"

She stopped, rolling her eyes and slowly turned to face him. The other members streamed past them. "See you at dinner," the vampire said as she passed the dragon.

The male nodded once, not taking his eyes off Cordia. This was bad. She could see by the look in his eyes that he was still hot for her... that he wanted more. That much was for sure. It warmed her and irritated her. He irritated her. Her reactions to him irritated her the most.

His eyes dipped down for a beat or two. Not in a way that made her feel uncomfortable but in a way that made her feel completely feminine and a whole lot attractive. For a couple of long, hard seconds, she was tempted to accept whatever it was he was about to offer. Oh, so very tempted.

Then again, all this male wanted was a warm snatch. By her estimation, they generally preferred a chase. Easy pickings were never as much fun. That's why he hadn't given the vampire a second glance. Even though the female was attractive. She had all of the attributes a male would want, including fertility. If the vamp backed off, just a little, she might just stand a chance.

Unfortunately, this particular male wanted a chase, followed by more sex. By the arrogant expression on his handsome face, she could see he expected to get it too.

Not happening.

One slip was enough. No more.

"I do not wish to engage with you, dragon." She began to turn away.

"Can I walk with you?"

"No." She shook her head. "I told you I don't like you."

His sexy half-smile was back. It only served to make him more attractive. A distraction she didn't need… or want. One she couldn't afford.

"You don't have to like me for me to walk with you." Those gorgeous eyes focused in on hers. They were such a strange color. His lashes were thick. His mouth full. Tar and feathers, but she was looking at his mouth.

"Suit yourself." She had meant to tell him to leave her alone but that had come out instead. Cordia picked up a fast pace, hoping he'd take the hint. Also, the sooner she could close and maybe even lock her door, the better. "I don't feel like talking to you either. We walk and that's it."

"I think we should order in together this evening. I don't much feel like mingling."

"I don't feel like mingling… at all. Not with anyone," she countered.

"Good thing I'm not 'anyone.' I know how your pussy tastes, so that makes me someone to you." He smirked at her when she glared at him. Even his stupid smirk was sexy. It made her feel tingly. That tightening in the pit of her stomach was back. Why did she have to be attracted to him? A dragon. Him. *No!* This didn't work for her. She preferred to be shunned. Maybe she should disclose a couple of important facts to him about herself. Ones that would change the way he looked at her. The dragon would look at her with disdain too.

Only.

Only.

Only…

She couldn't. Cordia didn't want him looking at her like that. It shouldn't matter and she shouldn't care, only she did and it did.

Blast.

Damn.

Cordia needed to get rid of him. "I don't feel like mingling with anyone or… with you. I most definitely don't feel like mingling with you. There!"

"Why do you have to be so… angry? Are you always this angry or is it just me?" His mouth turned up at one corner. Not quite a smile but close.

"I'm not angry… I'm a serious person. This conference is serious. What happened earlier was a… mistake."

"No, it wasn't." He frowned. Even that looked great. His eyes darkened, becoming more intense. He got these two lines between his brows. "We discussed it first. No mistake. There was no tripping or falling. My cock didn't accidentally slip into your very tight, very…"

"You can stop." She held up a hand, widening her eyes, trying hard to keep her breathing normal, her facial expression normal. She hoped and prayed to all the gods that he couldn't scent arousal.

They were close to her nest… her acco-mo-da-tion while here. A strange word. Nest was so much easier. "You know what I mean by mistake. I told you, the itch has been…" *What was the right word?* "It's been taken care of."

"Are you sure of that?"

"Yes!" It came out more harshly than she intended.

"I think you protest far too much and with far too much venom."

They arrived at her door. "Go find the vampire. She wants to make lots of shifter young and ideally with you."

He choked out a laugh. "I'd rather stay here with you."

Rather.

Not 'forget it' or "no way.' *Rather.* The dragon was a bastard. Just like most males she knew.

"I would *rather* you left me alone." Not much of a comeback. They arrived at her door.

"No can do, *partner.*" He leaned up against the wall next to the door. "Let me in. We can…" He smiled. "I would suggest talk but you already said you had nothing to say to me. Maybe I could change your mind about that."

It was her turn to laugh. It held zero humor. "No chance. Go away." She opened the door. Walked into the nest and shut it behind her, half expecting him to stop her somehow. The door slammed shut with a bang. She waited a few beats, almost waiting for him to knock but it never happened. Why did she feel disappointed? She was stupid. So idiotic. This was so much better. Then she thought about that word 'rather' and what it signified. For a moment she was tempted to let him in. To call him back if he was walking away. 'If'… stupid to use that word, of course he was walking away. Instead, she turned the lock with a definite click.

CHAPTER 6

"That poor dragon." The vampire shook her head. "You really hurt him. I've never heard such a racket. Lexi," she looked over at the wolf shifter, "mentioned how the poor male limped to his room after he left you."

Cordia sucked in a breath. She quickly schooled her features. *Had she hurt the male?* She hadn't thought so. At least, he had seemed fine. Maybe all the loud roars, grunts and shouts had been cries of pain. It was possible. *No! It couldn't be.*

A Feral's snatch could hold onto a male. A snatch was designed to take seed after all. It was designed to get it and to take it. As much as possible. Mounting followed by a short period of coupling where the male was unable to pull away. All designed to procreate. A parody. A cruel joke. Procreate. Right.

Not her.

The whole process was also designed to entice and to please. To give maximum pleasure to the male, so that more seed could be extracted. She doubted very much that the roars had been those born of agony. Why had he sniffed around again after the conference if he didn't want more of the same? This female was confused.

"Yes, he was quite badly hurt." Lexi nodded vigorously. "He was leaning quite heavily on the dragon female, limping even. I'm sure you didn't mean to hurt him?" She looked at Cordia, even tipping her head to the side in question.

Had she broken him somehow? *Maybe.* He hadn't complained. He'd even asked her for more. That wasn't the action of a male in pain. "He is a big, strong male and was perfectly fine when I left him." She took a bite of her bacon sandwich, hoping the conversation would end there. Then she had a thought; had the dragon said something to this female? Maybe they had spent time together the evening before. She took another bite of her meal trying not to think about it. It didn't matter and it was none of her business.

"Didn't look fine to me." Lexi shook her head.

"Poor thing probably needs some TLC," the vampire added, licking her lips. "I have heard somewhere that dragon blood is quite delicious."

"You want to help him by drinking his blood?" Cordia grimaced. She wasn't sure what TLC was but by the look in the vampire's eyes, she was sure it involved plenty of touching.

"Doesn't sound much like helping to me," Surora said as she sat down next to her.

Cordia had never been happier to see a fellow Feral.

She wasn't necessarily friendly with the other female, but it was nice to see a familiar face. Someone in her corner. These others were most definitely… 'enemy' was too strong a word, but it wasn't far off.

"I'd like to do more than just drink his blood," the vampire purred. "It was nice of them to send us a male to keep us company."

"Us?" Cordia frowned, taking another bite of her food. Why was she even responding to this creature?

"Yes, us," the shifter said, with a sly smile "You've had him. It's our turn. Don't you agree, Helga?"

So the male hadn't mounted the vampire… yet. Cordia didn't like these females. She hoped he stayed away from them. He could mount whomever he wanted, of course. She ultimately didn't care, but these two rubbed her the wrong way.

The vampire nodded. "Absolutely. I definitely want a turn with a male like that. He's quite delectable."

"Don't be greedy, Feral," the shifter added. "We want a turn as well. You were right…" She bit down on her bottom lip for a moment or two. "He is very attractive and has a lovely looking cock. Long with decent girth."

"My name is Cordia. You will address me as such." She was done playing games with these females. They could have the dragon for all she cared. Her itch was lanced… scratched, whatever the correct term. It wasn't necessarily one he created, but rather, one that had grown from going too long without rutting.

"Don't be so testy." The shifter looked put out. "We need to work together and build interspecies relationships."

"You can start by remembering my name." Cordia

narrowed her eyes on the female.

The shifter's eyes widened. "I did remem—"

"Good morning." The dragon sauntered in. His hair was still wet. He had this wide smile that made his eyes glint in the bright morning light. His chest was bare. His silver marking gleamed against hard muscles.

Everyone in the room said their good mornings back. The vampire actually fluttered her eyes. The shifter female, Lexi, was loud about it. They gave him a definite once over as he approached. Thankfully the elven females seemed unaffected. The panther and bear shifters smiled broadly but didn't look taken aback. Not that it mattered. Who cared how the others acted, or what the dragon did. It was none of her business. He could rut every female in attendance for all she cared.

Cordia couldn't bring herself to say anything in response to his bright hello. Instead, she took another mouthful of her meal. She planned to keep her head down and her mind on the conference.

The dragon looked around the table. There were two open seats. One next to her and one next to the vampire, who tapped the chair as soon as she saw him looking.

She tapped.

Two solid little beats that seemed to ring around the room. The dragon looked at her, completely serious all of a sudden. Those jewel-like eyes boring into her. "Good morning, Cordia."

She clenched her jaw and pulled in a breath, releasing it slowly. "I told you to call me Feral."

The shifter put down her glass with a clunk. "But you told us we had to—"

"I think I'll sit over," he plonked himself next to her,

"here." His plate was filled with what looked like everything from the breakfast table. He put down a glass of orange juice as well. He grinned at her. "Sleep well?"

"How are you feeling today, Stone?" The vampire wouldn't let up, she leaned forward staring down the table at him.

"Great." He kept his eyes on Cordia. "Never better," he added. "I'm ready to get started, looking forward to working on solutions to the fertility issues."

Cordia couldn't help the snort that was pulled from her.

"Something you wanted to say, Fera... Cordia," the shifter female asked, her gaze moving to her plate as soon as Cordia looked her way.

"The dragon has plenty of seed – I can attest to that firsthand – and therefore, he has nothing he needs to discuss with the group about fertility issues."

The male put his fork down with a clang. "I assure you... all of you," the male looked from one female to the next, "that I take these proceedings very seriously." He looked at her, keeping his eyes on her. "I want solutions to be found. I mean that." He spoke directly to her now, his voice deep and urgent. "I do understand the plight and the feelings of females suffering from infertility."

"I believe you." The shifter female smiled.

"Me too." The vampire winked at him.

It all made Cordia feel queasy. She picked up her napkin off her lap and wiped her mouth. Then she pushed back her chair and left. She needed to mentally prepare for the day ahead.

CHAPTER 7

Half an hour later...

"I know you are all eager to know what I have planned for you this morning." She widened her eyes, sucking in a deep breath. "We're going to start off the day with a team-building exercise." Gazelle was practically beaming.

This was bullshit! They had yet to discuss anything surrounding infertility.

"This is all about working together with your teammate. About overcoming adversity," Gazelle went on.

"What about the topic at hand?" Stone asked. "We need to—"

"After the team-building we'll break for lunch and commence with more formal discussions. We're going to play a little game this morning, called capture the flag."

The vampire, Helga, put up her hand. "Can we swap partners for the team-building?" She looked directly at him as she spoke. The funny thing was, that although Cordia could snap him like a twig, he was more afraid of the vampire, who was small and weak by comparison.

"No." Gazelle shook her head. "You need to stay with your partner."

Thank god!

He stepped in closer to Cordia, who looked at him like he was a piece of shit under her shoe. "This is stupid," she remarked.

"I agree, but we have to do it anyway." He spoke under his breath.

"I don't feel like working together with you," she whispered. "Or team-building. Or any of this. How is this even going to help us solve our fertility problems?" She mirrored his thinking.

"However," Gazelle went on, speaking a little louder and looking pointedly at them. "I am going to divide you into two teams. You guys are on one team." She pointed to some of the group. It included the vampire, Helga, and that shifter female who kept looking at him like he was a piece of meat. "The rest of you are Team Two." He sighed in relief when he realized the wolf shifter and the vampire were on the other team.

"That's not fair," Lexi remarked.

"Why not, Lexi?" Gazelle asked.

"They get him." She pointed at him. "A male. He's stronger. They'll win."

"They also have a Feral," Lexi added.

"You have a Feral too," Surora remarked, looking down at herself. "Last time I checked I wasn't chopped liver."

"I agree with Lexi. They have a male on their side.

Males are stronger than females. It is a proven fact. We want the male too. We insist on getting him. Maybe we can share." She winked at Cordia who ignored them flat. The vampire looked at him like she wanted to eat him rather than to have him on her team.

"You heard Gazelle." Cordia stepped forward. She wore another tank top – this one was dusty pink – and cut off jean shorts that showcased her thighs to perfection. "The teams have already been allocated. Deal with it!"

"We don't feel it's fair." The shifter stepped forward and folded her arms.

"We can beat you easily even if—" Cordia started.

"Of course you can," the vampire snorted, cutting her off, "you have him." She pointed at Stone with one of her long, painted nails.

"I wasn't finished," Cordia spat. "We can beat you with both his hands tied behind his back." She pointed a thumb at Stone.

"We don't need to go to such extreme measures," Gazelle began, looking shocked. "This is supposed to be fun."

"Yeah, surely we…" he also chimed in. Not loving the idea of having his hands tied behind his back.

"That's a fantastic idea, Feral." The vampire grinned, showing off gleaming fangs.

Cordia made a screeching noise, her eyes narrowed on Helga. "I told you my name. Best you use it!"

"Cordia… okay? Fine! You don't need to be quite so sensitive. I like your idea. The male must have his hands tied behind his back." She smiled at him, her eyes glinting deviously.

"Are you okay with that, Stone?" Gazelle asked,

looking concerned.

He glanced at Cordia, who nodded once.

"I guess so." He shrugged, still not loving the idea but then again, it was only a stupid game.

"I don't like it." Gazelle shrugged. "No violence is permitted, so I'm not sure, with that in mind, why we need to tie Stone up."

"Stone heads up our lair defense," Topaz chimed in. "He is the most senior team leader and responsible for combat and defense training of all of the males in our lair. I think he should be handicapped. It would be the fair thing to do." She grinned at him.

"Thanks for that." Stone couldn't help but smile. The she-dragon was on the other team. She was giving him shit.

Topaz shrugged, smiling broadly. "My pleasure." She winked at Stone, tossing out a laugh.

"See," the vampire looked him up and down for the tenth time that morning, her eyes seemed to brighten and her fangs seemed even longer than before, "further proof that he needs to be tied."

"Okay, okay. The male will be tied," Gazelle conceded. "Each team will receive a flag. You need to guard your flag while attempting to retrieve the flag of your opposition." She pulled in a breath before continuing. "The game is about stealth and tactics, *not* about strength. If you are caught trying to steal the flag or are found to be in the possession of the flag while still on enemy territory you can be sent to a cage. The opposition must tag you though." She made quote signs with her hands when she said cage. "Not a real cage. It's a designated area highlighted on the maps you'll get shortly. Each territory has its own cage area. If tagged, the offender must then sit inside the cage for a full fifteen minutes. Then they must return back to their own territory before attempting to steal the flag again." She licked her lips. "Keep in mind that if you are too hung up on defense, you will never capture the opposition's flag. Alternately, if you are too eager, you might lose your own flag. It's very much a balancing act. Working as a team is essential."

"Okay then." The vampire clapped her hands together. "I have silver-infused handcuffs." Helga grinned at Stone. "I think they'll work better than rope. This is going to be fun." She rubbed her hands together.

What the fuck?

"Don't worry." The vamp must have caught his horrified look. "They are lightly infused, so they won't make you sick. You will not be able to get free however." She winked at him.

"I honestly don't think that's necessary." Gazelle shook her head. "Being tied up and in hand-cuffs are not the same."

"How do we know he plays fair?" the wolf, Lexi asked, eyebrows raised.

"I'll give my word," Stone said, starting to feel irritated, "that's how."

"Actually," Topaz piped up, "I agree. Stone should be cuffed." She choked out a laugh.

"Whose side are you on?" Stone asked, frowning.

"Theirs," Topaz chuckled. "This *is* a competition after all."

"Rope, silver hand-cuffs," Cordia remarked. "It makes no difference. We will beat you regardless." The female looked just as irritated as he did. In fact, her hands were fisted. Her jaw tight and those gorgeous eyes were blazing. Cordia was ready to whip some ass.

"Remember," Gazelle said, sensing frayed nerves. "No violence! No shifting allowed either. The first team to get the opposition's flag back onto your own territory wins!" She handed out some printouts. "Both territories are clearly marked. Flag locations are marked but only for your own. You have fifteen minutes to strategize and then it's game on. When the opposition flag is slotted in place, a buzzer will sound, that way we'll know who wins in the end, even if it's a race to the finish. Good luck! You may begin strategizing now." She glanced at her watch.

"Let's get to our flag." Stone glanced at the other team. He could practically see ears flapping. His own senses were on high alert. Trying to pick any little tidbit that could help them. "We'll talk when we get there," he added when one of the elves tried to say something. "Safer that way." Not all of the species had superior hearing. They may not realize how easy it would be for opposite team members to pick up on strategies.

"Aren't you forgetting something, dragon?" Helga rattled a pair of cuffs between two fingers. They glinted in the sunlight.

"Give them to me." Cordia held out her hand.

The vampire made a sound of disagreement, her eyes on him. "No way! I will secure them myself." She smirked as she walked over to him. "Turn around, hands together."

Stone glanced over at Cordia who was already walking in the direction of their territory, to where the flag would be. He winced as Helga closed the cuffs. They clicked as they sealed around his wrists, not giving him much room for movement.

"We can't have you escaping, now can we?" Helga purred. "I'm coming for you," she whispered.

"Don't you mean the flag?" he asked, looking back over his shoulder as he began to walk.

She winked. "Of course. I look forward to our little game."

"By our, you mean the teams."

"Absolutely." She winked.

Stone jogged to catch up. The others in his team held back slightly, looking back over their shoulders waiting for him. Cordia kept on forging ahead. Stone picked up the pace to meet up with them. The cuffs already irritated him, but he'd deal. It took them five minutes walking at a brisk pace to get far enough away from the other team.

"Hold up!" Stone yelled at Cordia's retreating back. "We only have ten minutes left before the game starts," he said as he glanced at his watch, having to pull his hands around to see his wrist. *Damn cuffs!* They gathered around him. "Let's decide on a strategy," Stone said.

Cordia turned. Her jaw was tight, her eyes focused. She looked both pissed and determined. "We need to win!" she stated, putting her hands on her hips.

"I agree," Stone said.

"Sounds good," the bear shifter acknowledged. They all formed a huddle.

"I'll defend our flag," Cordia stated. She narrowed her eyes, which shone in the morning light, giving them a gorgeous honeyed glow.

"You couldn't use force or aggression though," the elf remarked. She must have picked up on Cordia's agitated state. It was hard to miss. "You would have to tap the person out, thus sending them to the cage."

"I know." Cordia nodded, looking resolute.

"No hard 'taps,'" the panther shifter snorted.

"I know… okay." Cordia clenched her jaw. "Let's get on with it."

"We need to be clever about this," Stone said. "We need to play to our strengths and be aware of our weaknesses."

"That sounds like a good idea," the same petit elf said, pulling hair behind her pointy ears. She smiled shyly as they turned back her way.

"Maybe each of us should highlight what we are good at," Stone said, glancing at her name badge. "We can start with you, Delfinia."

The elf nodded deeply. "Elves do not have greatly superior senses like the other species, and the females do not have much in the way of strength. I am great with a bow and arrow… not that it will help us with this challenge." She giggled, her cheeks turning pink.

"Thank you." Stone nodded. "What about you?" he asked the panther shifter.

"My senses are fantastic," Willow announced. "I'm strong, fast and silent."

Another teammate introduced herself. "I'm a vampire. My name is Penelope." She pointed at her badge. "I have fantastic senses. I'm strong and fast."

"Bonnie," a tall, dark-haired female stepped forward. "I'm a bear shifter. I'm not as fast as some of you will be, but my senses are great and I'm really strong." She flexed her biceps.

Finally, Cordia stepped forward. "I have excellent vision. I am also strong. Not that it will help much in this instance. I'm also fast. I think I should guard our flag. I will be good at defending." She cracked the knuckles on her right hand.

"Thank you all," Stone said. "I have excellent senses. I am strong and fast." He looked from one female to the next. "I am unfortunately handicapped." He turned, showing off his cuffs. "My suggestion is that you use me as a decoy. I will pretend to be out looking for the flag. I'll be captured, hence occupying one or two of the other team, making for an opening to capture their flag. I will work hard at holding the opposition's attention for as long as possible."

"That's a great idea." The panther shifter's dark eyes seemed to lighten. "If Cordia and one of the others – Delfinia maybe – guards our flag, then Penelope and I will head for *their* flag." The panther shifter pointed at the vampire female. "Bonnie can patrol our territory, sending any trespassers to the cage." Willow pointed at the bear shifter who nodded.

"I agree, however, I think that Cordia…" His eyes locked with hers. "You should go with Willow to retrieve the flag. I think that a bear shifter will do better guarding."

"I don't have great hearing." Cordia shook her head. "I could be captured."

"You have the best vision," Stone replied. "Willow can be your ears."

"I have great vision too," the panther shifter announced, looking mildly put out.

"I know, but not like a Feral… I assure you. Nothing beats a Feral in that regard. Also, Feral are fantastic where stealth is concerned. I doubt any of the species comes close. The two of you," he nodded in the direction of the elf and bear, "will need to watch for the Feral on the other team. She'll be in and out and you won't even know it."

"He is right." Cordia nodded. "Surora is greatly proficient as a warrior."

"Yeah, but I'll scent her from—" the bear began, a deep frown marring her forehead.

Stone shook his head. "Feral have *no* scent. Well, mostly no scent." He winked at Cordia who narrowed her eyes. The only time she'd had any kind of scent was when she was turned on. Then she'd been fucking delectable.

It looked like she knew exactly what he was thinking because she frowned and looked away.

Stone needed to get his head out of his ass at once. As much as he enjoyed thinking of their time together, he needed to concentrate. They all did. Stone glanced at his watch. "We have a minute to finalize this. I'll be a decoy. The elf and the vampire will watch the flag. The Feral and the panther will take the opposition flag, while the bear is on general lookout. If we catch them in our territory, we have to touch them to send them to the cage for fifteen minutes."

"Don't worry, I'm fast," the vampire announced, narrowing her eyes. "They won't get anywhere near our flag."

"I'm fast too." The elf held her head high. "I forgot about that." She giggled, looking shy all over again.

"That's perfect." Stone nodded. "Is everyone in agreement?" He specifically looked Cordia's way. He believed she could win this thing for them.

The Feral finally nodded, keeping her face impassive.

"You three head out then," he spoke to the defenders, who nodded and jogged away. Stone looked down at the map in his hands, holding it out to Cordia and Penelope.

"Their flag could be anywhere. I'm going to guess that it's either here," he pointed to a section of the valley, "or here. Simply because these areas would be easier to defend. What do you think?"

"Agreed." Penelope nodded.

He went on when Cordia didn't comment. "I'll head out this way." He pointed it out on the map. "I'll clunk around and then fall or something. Not hard to do when your hands are behind your back." He half-smiled.

The vampire laughed.

"That should give the two of you the opening you need." He smiled at Cordia who nodded. "You listen out, Penelope. Let's do this."

"We got this." The vamp nodded, looking resolute.

"We will finish them!" Cordia announced. With that, she turned and began running in the direction of the flag. Moving in a fast but steady pace. Her footfalls silent. The vampire gave him a questioning look and then raced after her. For a moment, Stone worried that he had perhaps made the wrong decision to send the Feral out there. Maybe he should have reminded her of the no violence rule again. It was too late to make changes now.

CHAPTER 8

C ordia hated this. The pressure was all-consuming. Stone had made it her responsibility to secure the flag. It was a responsibility she was taking seriously.

They had to win this.

They had to!

It almost felt like it was her against the two of them. Helga and Lexi. Cordia ground her teeth. Stone's fan club. It shouldn't matter to her, but it did. She wanted to beat them. Break them. Destroy them. She fisted her hands as she ran. Also, she had a competitive streak a mile long. It was how it was.

"Wait up," the vampire whispered. "I'm supposed to be your ears. We will need to slow down soon."

The vampire spoke too much. The female made altogether too much noise.

Cordia put up her hand and slowed. Penelope fell in next to her. Cordia put her finger to her lips gesturing for silence. Noise could travel far in this type of environment.

The female gestured for her to slow down, she lifted her eyes, seeming to listen to something.

Cordia knew that they were making good time, a few more minutes and they would be in the vicinity of the first potential flag location. She searched all around them, not spotting anything out of the ordinary. Cordia pointed at her ears. Had the other female heard something out of the ordinary?

The vampire nodded her head… she lifted her eyes for a few seconds, then she smiled.

Cordia frowned.

"Stone is being noisy," Penelope mouthed to Cordia. "I could hear him falling all the way here." She laughed noiselessly.

Cordia nodded, hoping that his plan worked. She sucked in a breath as she noticed movement in the distance. She gestured to the vampire, then pointed at her eyes and over at the far ridge. Penelope nodded and they both hid behind an outcrop of bushes and trees. Cordia narrowed her eyes, spotting Lexi and Helga. They were headed in Stone's direction. Moving fast. Why did it have to be them? They were going to head him off. This was the chance she and Penelope had been hoping for. Two of the other team were now occupied.

Cordia should be happy. Stone would be a definite distraction. Particularly to those two females. They could get the flag now. At least, they'd have more of a chance. Penelope's eyes tracked the two of them as they headed off in the male's direction. She gave Cordia the thumbs up.

Cordia nodded. They waited until the females were far

enough away and then continued, moving as fast as the terrain would allow. Every now and then, a rock tumbled or a twig cracked. Maybe Stone had been right. Penelope wasn't quiet at all. The Feral were far more superior at stealth while on the move.

All of a sudden, Penelope came to a halt... she seemed to be listening to something.

"What?" Cordia mouthed.

"Stone." She lifted her eyes. "They have him." Then she smiled broadly. What was there to smile about? They needed to move.

She pointed in the direction they were going, to signal to the vampire to keep going.

Penelope rolled her eyes and gave a shake of the head. "Looks like they want to play with him," she mouthed. "Those two." She shook her head.

Play!

"Play?" Cordia knew exactly what the vampire was hinting at. It made her stomach churn. "What about the game? What about winning?"

The other female shrugged. "They are more interested in him." She bobbed her brows. "He is flirting back," she mouthed. "I'm sure he's just distracting them for us." Penelope grinned. "We'd better get going." She began walking in the direction they had been headed in. "We need to take this opportunity." She picked up the pace again.

Cordia gripped the female's shoulder. Her heart pounding. "What if he isn't actually interested?" she mouthed. The male's hands were cuffed behind his back. It could get nasty.

Penelope shook her head. "What male in his right mind

would refuse two females?"

"He might." Cordia tended to agree with Penelope though. It made her feel funny inside, thinking of him with the two of them. Thinking of how smug they would be afterward.

"Leave him. He's doing his job," she mouthed.

"He might not be interested."

She cocked her head. "I think he is."

For a second she was tempted to leave him. Species males were all the same after all. Dragons included. Stone among them. He had proven that yesterday with her. The male was strong enough and mature enough to take care of himself. Stone didn't need her. She shouldn't get involved. She should focus on her objective. Secure the flag. He was quite capable of…

Was he capable of taking care of himself right then?

Cuffed in silver. He wouldn't be able to change into his animal form even if he wanted to. Cordia needed to find out. If she was wrong, she'd leave them to it but if she was right, she couldn't just leave him like that. At the mercy of those bitches. Stone was part of the team. He was her partner at this conference. She needed to at least find out. Besides, that feeling inside her had worsened. The thought of him with the females made her feel ill.

Cordia tapped Penelope on the side of the arm. "I'm going to help him. You get the flag." She ignored the other female's shocked expression and headed to where she guessed they would be.

Cordia picked up the pace, concentrating on staying completely silent. She kept scanning the vegetation for any enemies, or for signs of the three. It didn't take her long to find them.

Cordia picked her way through the foliage. She would assess and decide what to do. The vampire straddled Stone, who was on his ass. He was using his cuffed hands to keep himself upright. His jaw was tight, his eyes blazed.

A lump rose in Cordia's throat. The wolf shifter stood on the edge of the clearing, facing away from the two on the ground. She seemed to be on lookout and was smiling. "Hurry up already," she whispered over her back. "I want my turn as well."

Bile rose up in her throat as Cordia moved in closer, careful not to allow her anger at these two females to cloud her judgment.

"You can just sit there, Stone. I will ride you." She tried to kiss him, but he turned his head.

"What is it? Don't you like me?"

"I like you just fine. You're a beautiful female. I'm not into kissing, that's all."

"It can be quite enjoyable. I'll show you." She tried to kiss him again, and again Stone turned away.

"No… I prefer straight out rutting."

Cordia could contest to that.

"Yes," the wolf hissed. "Get to it. We don't have much time."

"That's just it," Stone said, sounding irritated. "Why a quick rut when we can have a good time. All three of us." He looked over at the wolf. "There would be no need for a lookout. My bed tonight. What do you females say?"

"I'm turned on now. I want you now," the vampire whined.

Cordia wanted to smack her face until she bled. She wanted to tear her beating heart out of her chest. That feeling was back. Cordia now recognized it for what it was.

Jealousy.

"I don't like rushed sex," Stone remarked, sounding casual.

"What was that yesterday with the Feral then?"

Cordia felt a hiss build in her throat but bit back.

"It was very average," Stone managed to sound bored.

What?

No!

The vampire choked out a laugh. "Of course it was. I want you now, dragon." The female put her hand between his legs and fisted his cock through his pants.

Cordia knew that she should turn around right then. She should leave. *No!* She needed to see this. It would stop these stupid wayward emotions she was having for this male. They were born out of loneliness. She realized that, but they needed to be halted.

"You're getting hard." The vampire sounded excited. "See, I told you a quickie would be enjoyable for you."

Stone growled. "Get off me!" His face got this pinched look, which was in opposition to what he was saying. He clenched his jaw, his eyes blazing, but this time, with more than just anger. It pissed her off. She couldn't say exactly why. "Later, vampire. I said I didn't want to rut now."

Her hand continued to work him. "If you lift your ass for a second or two, I'll slip your pants off and—"

Stone snarled. "Get the fuck off me!"

"Admit that you want this dragon. You were flirting with me not five seconds ago. You told me how pretty I am. That you think I have great breasts."

"Get off me," Stone growled. He squeezed his eyes shut, making a noise of frustration. There was an edge to the noise that had her hackles going up. The male was getting aroused. He may not like it at this point, but it didn't mean it wasn't happening.

Maybe she should leave. Cordia took a step back.

"You, like all species males, like to fuck. You proved that yesterday with the Feral. Don't try to deny that you want this. I can see it on you. I can scent it on you. Your cock is lovely and hard. It wouldn't be that way if— Here…" She pulled her shirt over her head. "The males of my kind find me attractive." She thrust out her chest. Cordia couldn't see from this angle, but she knew the female was attractive. She really should leave. Cordia took another step back. "You said you find me attractive. I'm desperate for you now. You can have the two of us tonight."

Stone's eyes stayed on the vampires. He didn't deny that the vampire was attractive. He didn't look at her mammary glands either. "You should be going after our flag," Stone tried. "This is a competition. Get dressed, get off me and—"

Maybe he was playing a game. Dragging this out just to keep them busy for longer? He was going to let her rut him in the end. The pinched look on his face told her so. Cordia really should leave them to it. The cloying feeling grew and grew.

"I have the only flag I want in this competition." Her hand stroked him again and Stone growled, his teeth clenched.

"Come and help me," Helga spoke over her shoulder to the wolf, Lexi.

"I mean it, Helga. We need to get back in the game," Stone tried again. "We'll rut later. I swear."

Helga laughed. "One quick rut," she purred. "The three of us can still get together tonight." She rubbed her chest up against his and tried to kiss Stone, who turned his head. He grimaced, his face was still pinched. Stone was definitely turned on. She could see it in that pinched look. Could hear it in the huskiness of his voice. If she had any kind of sense of smell, she'd pick it up with her nose as well.

Cordia's hands were so tightly clenched that her fingers hurt. She wasn't sure what to do. This was a male. His blood ran with testosterone. His urges were to fuck.

"Help me," Helga asked the wolf again.

"Why should I?" the wolf spat. "I can see you don't plan on giving me a turn."

Like Stone was a carnival ride.

"Tonight, sweet wolf," Helga purred.

"I don't want to wait that long," Lexi huffed.

"Come and help me. I can't get his pants off without ripping them. Should I rip them, dragon?"

Stone growled low. "Why don't—"

Lexi turned towards the couple on the floor, giving Cordia the gap she needed. Besides, she'd seen enough. This whole scene sickened her.

Cordia raced into the clearing and shoved the wolf hard, sending her flying. There was a crack as her skull connected with a thick tree trunk. Cordia heard the female collapse.

She kicked Helga, who was still straddling Stone. The vampire went flying in a spray of blood and what looked like several of her teeth. *Good!*

Cordia crouched down next to Stone. "Are you alright?"

The male grinned at her. "I am now. Thank—"

Cordia didn't wait to hear anymore. She jumped up and headed back to where Penelope would be. Moving quickly and quietly, continually scanning the undergrowth for signs of movement. Cordia checked her watch. By now, the vampire would have been on the return path, if she had found the flag in the first location. Unless, of course, she'd been tagged, which was a distinct possibility since Cordia had left her to fend for herself. Hopefully, she was en route to the second location.

Cordia was unsure of what to do for a few seconds.

Making a decision, she changed direction, heading for the second location. Minutes later she spotted something moving fast to the far right of her. It was Penelope. She was sprinting, with two members of the other team hot on her heels. Penelope was breathing heavily, hair stuck to her brow. Her cheeks were bright red from the exertion.

Cordia went after them. She was still fresh and caught up to Penelope easily, having to sidestep the panther, who tried to tap her out.

"Help!" Penelope gasped. She was more exhausted than Cordia had realized. On the verge of collapse. "Here." The female handed the flag to Cordia who nodded, taking over. The elf and the panther ignored Penelope as she slowed. They followed the flag. They chased her. Cordia picked up speed.

She leaped over fallen logs, dodging trees and bushes, clutching the flag tightly in her hand. Cordia could hear that she was losing them. She kept her eyes wide open, afraid of being ambushed on her way back. She was still on the opposition's territory. If she was tapped, she'd end up in time-out.

Her arms pumped and she took deep breaths. Cordia spotted movement to her left. It was the dragon female, coming at her hard. Face set in determination. The female had been lying in wait and was fresh. She moved with surprising speed. Cordia pushed herself, climbing up the side of a rocky ridge before picking up the pace. She heard rocks clatter as the other female came after her. Too close on her heels for comfort. Cordia was fast but she wasn't as fresh as the dragon. She forced herself to push harder. The border was less than a minute away. Once she crossed it, she'd be safe. Her only goal would be to get the flag back to the starting point before the other team.

There was another flash of movement. This time from the right. Someone else coming to head her off. Her heart sank. She wasn't sure she could outrun two. *Oh no!* Not someone to head her off. It was worse. It was Surora. The female had the flag and was headed back to their starting point. It was a race between the two of them and Surora was ahead. Cordia's heart beat faster. Using every ounce of strength she possessed, she raced for the finish.

The dragon stopped dead as soon as they reached the border. There was no point for her to keep up the chase. Cordia was back on their own territory but instead of slowing, she pushed harder. Her lungs burned. Her heart pumped, feeling like it might explode. She thought about Helga and Lexi. Anger churned in her gut when she thought about the dragon. About all he had said. She had to win this. *Had to!*

Cordia passed the bear shifter who jumped up and down, yelling words of encouragement. Cordia couldn't hear over the pounding of blood pumping through her veins. She could see the finish. Cordia raced on, slotting the flag into the holder provided. A shrill bell sounded.

Cordia bent over at the waist. She had a stitch on her right side and clamped a hand over the area, panting hard. Sweat dripped.

"Wow!" the bear remarked. "That was some running. I don't think I've ever seen anyone move that fast." Her eyes were wide, they burned with excitement.

Cordia pulled herself upright, mouth dry. She nodded once. "Thank you."

"We won!" The bear clapped her hands. "I can hardly believe it. Surora had a lead. She's fast but you still beat her. You must feel amazing."

Cordia forced a smile. She nodded. "I am very happy!" Why didn't she feel ecstatic? She wanted to win, and she had.

Stone.

The male.

He was messing with her head. She should never have gone to his 'rescue.' *Asshole!*

"Don't look so disappointed," the bear added. "You did well. You can be proud. We won!"

Cordia forced a smile. "Thank you. I do feel proud. I'm just a little tired."

They began making their way back to where Gazelle was waiting. The vampire smiled.

"We did it." Penelope tapped Cordia on the back. The female was glowing.

"Yes, we did!" Cordia tapped the female on the side of the arm. "All of us." Everyone except Stone that was. She clenched her teeth, trying to tamp down her irritation. It wasn't entirely true. He had done his bit. She still felt jealous. Of a dragon. Of him. A player. That's all he was and yet here she was, unable to enjoy this moment. She didn't have real feelings for the male. She didn't even know him, and he was… he was a dragon. Not even one of her own kind. It was baffling.

More and more members of the two teams gathered together. They all congratulated her, or each other. The losing members commiserated as well. And then there he was. The male in question sauntered up. His hands still cuffed behind his back. It didn't take away from how imposing he was. How tall. How broad his chest was. His smile was a mile wide and as arrogant as any she had ever seen. "Those are some legs." His gaze dipped down to her thighs and her belly tightened. *Arghhh!* She didn't like reacting to him. He didn't deserve her jealousy. He didn't deserve any part of her.

"Congratulations!" he chuckled. "I don't think I've ever seen anyone move like that."

"The other team had the lead and you still did it," the bear gushed. "I've never seen anything like it either."

"I had no chance of catching you." Topaz shook her head. "I sure as hell tried."

"You did well, dragon," Cordia spoke to the female.

Topaz smiled and nodded her head. "Not well enough."

"Well done, guys," Gazelle began. "It looks like Cordia's team are the winners. They—"

"Wait just a second." Helga walked up. Her neck and chest were bloody. Her shirt was glued down in parts by congealed blood. Her hair was a mess. Cordia noticed with satisfaction that there were definitely teeth missing. It looked like at least three, including one of her fangs. She finally felt like she had won. Her victory was short-lived though.

Lexi had a gash on her forehead that was scabbing over. She had dried blood dripping down her face.

Gazelle gasped. "What happened to the two of you?"

"She," Helga pointed at Cordia, "happened. The Feral did this."

Cordia narrowed her eyes, biting her tongue to hold back a hiss.

"They don't deserve the win," Lexi added. "She used excessive force during the game. She broke the no violence rule. Look at me. I lost a fang, for blood's sake."

"That's not true," Cordia said. "I can explain. It wasn't like that."

Helga folded her arms. "Please do explain. I, for one, would love to hear it."

"I was helping Stone. They were…" She stopped there.

"We were what?" Helga smirked.

Flirting with Stone, who was flirting back. About to have sex with Stone, who was inviting them round to his place later for more of the same. Helga had been feeling the male up. What was she going to say exactly? That she felt the need to rescue him from them? That she was jealous? She'd be the laughingstock.

Cordia glanced at Stone who was looking at the sky, and then at something on the far horizon. It was clear she wasn't going to get help from him. *Bastard!* If she gave the real reason for attacking the females she'd look like an idiot. Who was she kidding? She *was* an idiot. "I did use excessive force. I don't always know my own strength, especially when pitted against such inferior, weak beings," she said, trying hard to remain calm.

"What?" Helga snorted. "How dare you say that?"

"Because it's true," Cordia shot back.

"You can't—" Lexi began.

"The rules are clear." Gazelle was frowning, she looked apologetic as well. "You used violence."

"I'm so sorry." Cordia shook her head, feeling terrible for her team.

"I don't accept the apology." Helga narrowed her eyes. "It's going to take a couple of days to grow back my teeth."

"I wasn't apologizing to you," Cordia threw back. "I was apologizing to them." Cordia looked at each of her teammates in turn. Avoiding Stone. She wished she'd left well enough alone. These three deserved each other. Stone was just like all the other males. He didn't give a shit about her. He had shown her some passing interest and she'd lapped it up like an abandoned puppy in a scrapyard.

"You will have to forfeit the game." Gazelle's features softened as she looked at Cordia and the rest of her team. For a moment she considered using her power to heal the two females. She didn't have much of anything left. Maybe not even enough, even though the injuries were minor.

Then the vampire gave her a dirty look. "I should hope so."

The other team made a show at celebrating but it was lackluster at best. Lexi and Helga made the most noise about it.

"It doesn't matter." Penelope shook her head. "It's just a game."

"Exactly," the little elf piped up. "We don't care." She shrugged her tiny shoulders.

"That was still some fantastic running," Stone said, but Cordia ignored him.

"You can all go and freshen up," Gazelle remarked. "Lunch will be served in an hour, followed by continued talks on the various fertility problems amongst the species."

Cordia headed for the nests. They were clustered together on ground level. Very claustrophobic. Very strange.

"Cordia!" Stone yelled. "Hey!" he shouted again. "Get these handcuffs off."

"I like the look on you," she heard Helga say.

Cordia refrained from rolling her eyes. She picked up the pace. As she rounded the corner to their accommodations, she spotted the dragon. He was still chasing after her. His hands still behind his back.

"Wait!"

Couldn't he take a hint? She kept going.

CHAPTER 9

"Hold up!" he yelled, just as she slammed the door closed, putting her back to the cool wood.

Ten seconds later and he knocked… and then again.

"Go away!" she groaned.

"We need to talk." He sounded calm and together, which irritated her.

"I don't want to talk to you!" she yelled, sounding like a child. She was acting like one too but couldn't seem to help it.

"Please. You can't leave me out here like this. I need help getting out of these." He rattled the cuffs. "I beg you. I'll go on my knees if you promise to open up. Give me ten minutes of your time. Just ten."

"Ten." She snorted. "That would be ridiculous. We don't have nearly enough to say to one another." She was also still sweaty and very much in need of a shower.

"I beg to differ, but I'll take seven minutes if that will

make you feel more comfortable."

"Seven?" She choked out a laugh. "What kind of a number is seven? I'll give you five tops, and only if you make the first ten seconds count."

"You're on!"

Cordia turned. What the hell was she doing? She just needed to stay as far away from this male as possible. Only, she couldn't very well do that since he was her partner for another two days. Best she get this over with. Cordia opened the door and folded her arms.

"Sheesh!" He smiled at her. "If looks could kill, I'd be cremated."

"You have five seconds before I slam this door in your face." Why was she so angry with him? She had no right. This needed to stop. Talking wasn't going to help. Cordia began shutting the door.

"Wait! I'm sorry. I want to apologize to you."

Blast! Now she would have to hear him out. She pushed out a breath and looked him in the eyes. Like jewels in the morning light. She wasn't sure what the name of the stone was. They were a deep purple contrasting sharply to his bronzed skin and sandy blond hair. "Speak," she urged him.

He got a pained expression. "Can I come in?"

She shook her head. Cordia didn't want him in her space.

"Will you at least remove the cuffs...please?" His eyes were pleading. He turned around, the keys were clutched in his hands.

"For once the vampire and I agree. They look good on you."

"Please... I..."

"Fine," she sighed the word.

His look of relief was almost comical.

She took the key and inserted it into the lock. The restraints made a clicking noise and they popped open. Stone rubbed his newly freed wrists. "That feels amazing." He rolled his shoulders and brought his arms up in front of him, swinging them back and forth.

"You were saying," Cordia urged him on. Why was she giving him a chance here?

"I apologize." Stone gripped the doorjamb above him with both hands. The male was so tall, he could reach easily, his arms were still bent.

She waited. "For not sticking up for me just now?" she finally blurted, when he didn't say anything more. "For being a horse's ass?"

"Yes, I did sound like a horse's ass." He nodded. "I am sorry, although I couldn't exactly stick up for you, now could I? You have to admit it." He smiled a really sexy half-smile. He leaned forward, closing the space between them. She wanted to take a step back but refrained from doing so. If she took even one small step, he'd technically be inside and then she would *really* have a hard time getting rid of him.

Cordia nodded. "You could have and should have stood up for me. You could have said something. Those females they… they…" She shook her head, her cheeks feeling hot. "Forget it! Just forget the whole thing. I should never have gone to that clearing. I should never have rescued you." She snorted. "Rescued." She rolled her eyes so hard she was sure she damaged a muscle. "You didn't need rescuing, now did you? Sexy background music would have been better for what was going on between

Helga and..." She winced, realizing how jealous she sounded. "I'm an idiot. A complete idiot. I lost the challenge for our team and it's all *your* fault. You should have said something back there... anything. Why are you even apologizing when you don't mean it? You should go now."

She started to shut the door, but he gripped it, holding on. The wood groaned. "Wait. I *am* sorry the whole incident happened. I'm sorry you saw... what you did. I'm sorry you heard what you did. I'm sorry I couldn't stand up for you. I'm sorry we won only to lose in the end." He looked to his left. "Please let me in so that we can talk about this properly. So that I can explain better."

"You've said what you needed to say. You should go now."

"No. I need to tell you the reason I didn't stand up for you."

"I don't want to hear it." She prayed to the gods he didn't know the real reason why she had done what she did. *Please! Please! Oh please!* It would kill her. He needed to leave. This needed to be over right then. She should never have rutted this male.

"Cordia..." His whole stance softened. "Hey..."

She didn't need his apologies or his sympathy. She fought to close the door. He kept his grip on the wood, which groaned some more. "You were jealous. That's why. You thought...."

She couldn't hold his gaze for a second longer. Embarrassment filled her, making her cheeks heat. Making her whole body burn with shame. What the hell was she doing messing with this male? Cordia let the door go and walked into the nest, turning on her heel when she realized he was following her. She pointed a finger at him. "Don't come in here, and that's not true. I was not... jealous." She whispered the word; her cheeks were on fire.

Stone closed the door behind him. It slammed shut with a definite bang. "You were. You still are... and I'm glad."

"I'm sure you're happy about it," she threw back at him before she could stop herself. "It must be wonderful having all these females throwing themselves at you. Well, you can take me off your little fan club list. I'm not interested."

"Don't say that. You *are* interested. You're very interested." He took another step towards her and this time she stepped back. His eyes perused her body for a second or two. "I am too, Cordia. Very fucking interested."

"No!" She shook her head so hard her hair went flying about her head. "No, you are not! This is all a big game to you."

"I am interested! Very much so. From the first time I laid eyes on you. It's no game. I'm serious. Whatever is brewing between us is serious."

She snorted. "That's why you told Helga sex with me was boring."

"I didn't mean it. Fuck! I was talking shit. Buying time."

"I call it being an ass. There is nothing between us. Furthermore, we've known each other all of five minutes. They haven't been all that great either. I still don't like you." She made a face. "We've pretty much been at each other's throats the entire time."

"It's been longer than five minutes and I disagree... we've been at more than each other's throats." He held her gaze, lifting his brows. The start of a grin lifting the one corner of his mouth.

She choked out a laugh. "That was nothing. Less than nothing. You said it yourself."

"I didn't mean it! It was something... we broke the table and didn't even know it had happened until we were done. That's more than fucking nothing... hell, it's more than just plain something."

"Look, I'm done with this conversation. We are not compatible."

"We fucking are!" he growled. "I told you I wanted more. I meant it."

"Only you want more with your whole fan club as well. You would have mounted those two..." she felt a shudder run through her, "them... the vampire and the wolf, if I hadn't... shown up."

"If you hadn't slapped them around in a jealous rage, you mean?" He pulled his lips into his mouth in an attempt to hold back a laugh.

She hissed at him. *The bastard!*

"Okay, okay..." He held up his hands, grinning. "I'm sorry. I'm stoked is all. Stoked that you would do that for me because I like you too. Very much."

"Yeah, right! You like me so much you were ready to let them jump you like—"

"I was going to allow no such thing. If you hadn't arrived when you did, I would have—"

"She had her hand on your prick!" Cordia yelled. "You were into it."

"I wasn't! I swear to god. I was playing along to buy time. When I saw things were about to get out of hand, I was going to put a stop to it, but I didn't have to because you saved the day. Thank you!" He cupped her cheeks. "You saved me and now I owe you... big time." Blast and damn, his eyes were focused on her lips. His gaze intense.

"You don't owe me anything." She moved away from his grasp. This felt... wrong but only because it felt... right. "You should go."

"Not on your life." He took a step towards her and she took a step back. He took another step. This time he reached out and grabbed her arm before she could move away. "Don't run. I want to get to know you. I want to spend time with you."

Oh hell! Feathers and tar. This was bad. "No!" she practically yelled. "We are from different species. It would never work."

"Didn't you read the agenda for this conference? Interspecies relations will be encouraged in future. It's one of the main topics up for discussion. Vampire females are able to have young with the shifters. Infertile females have had young with elves. You never know how things will turn out if we—"

"I can't... it won't work... I—"

"We're getting ahead of ourselves." He spoke in a soothing voice. "I met you yesterday for claw's sake. Non-humans are quick but not that damned quick. We have until the end of the conference to get to know each other better and then maybe—"

"No! No way."

"Okay fine." He ran his hand up and down the side of her arm. "We can enjoy our two days together. Let's not even think of beyond for now."

"I don't think it's a good idea if—"

His eyes narrowed into hers. "Let's not think beyond

the next hour then. Would that work for you?" He didn't wait for her response. "We have forty-five minutes before we are needed back for lunch. Let's talk."

She shot him a look in answer to his question.

"Okay, no talking." He shrugged. "Maybe we could take a shower together? I'd like to wash more than just your back." He slid his arm around her waist and pulled her against him.

"Not a good idea," she stammered. His chest was hard, pressing firmly against her breasts. She arched her back, gripping his biceps, which were hard and thick.

"You're right. It would take too damned long to get all the way to the bathroom. I like the way you think, Feral." His eyes were focused on her lips. Before Cordia could do or say anything, he covered her mouth with his. His tongue parted her lips and clashed with hers. His lips were soft. The kiss was both rough and passionate. It was both soft and soothing, hot as the deepest depths of Hades.

Cordia moaned, entwining her fingers into the hair at the nape of his neck. The fingers of her other hand dug into the hard muscles of his back. The kiss seared her. It undid her. She couldn't get enough of the sexy dragon. She should push him away, but she couldn't. She found herself pulling him closer. Moaning into his mouth. Giving back just as much as she took.

Cordia whimpered when Stone broke the kiss. She didn't think she'd ever whimpered before in her life. Not for anyone or anything. "I thought you didn't like kissing." The notion entered her mind from nowhere. This was not a male who did not enjoy kissing.

"I told you. That was a bunch of bullshit. I like kissing just fine as long as it's with the right female." To prove a point, he brushed his lips over hers.

His eyes were narrowed into hers and his jaw was tight. If it wasn't for the desire in his eyes, she would've believed that he was angry. His whole body radiated raw tension. His muscles bulged. He even growled, long and low as his hands tightened around her.

Her heart leaped to her throat and excitement coursed through her veins. He picked her up – as in off the floor – which was no small feat considering that she was a Feral. She was heavy. Her beast was large and powerful and tucked in beneath her human skin. He made the smallest grunting noise as he began to walk.

The gasp she made was swallowed as his mouth covered hers. His tongue clashed with hers once again and the sound of ripping filled the room. Cool air abraded her very wet snatch as he tore off her shorts. She wrapped her arms around his neck, her heart racing.

There was no time to think or even to breathe as her back hit the wall, her ass rested on something cool. "Put your legs around my hips. I need to be inside of you." He nipped at her lower lip, sending shockwaves through her body. Her clit throbbed. Her breasts felt heavy.

She did as he said, locking her ankles behind him. Then remembered that she might break him and pulled back. "Careful," she warned. "I might hurt you."

"I need you so badly," Stone moaned as he pushed his hand between them using a finger to rub on her clit. It was at total odds with what he had just said. Cordia expected him to just mount her, but she didn't care because his touch felt so damned good.

Her head fell back slightly, and her mouth dropped open. Her breath came in ragged pants which turned to a loud moan when he pushed a finger inside her.

"You're so fucking wet," he said as he pulled his cotton pants down. His face was pinched. His eyes glowed. His jaw was tight.

His prick sprang free, long and thick. It turned her on even more, seeing the desperation etched into his features. This time he breached her with two fingers, pushing in and out of her in slow even strokes that made her cry out.

"Are you ready for me?" he asked, his voice deep.

She looked down, seeing the head of his thick cock pressed between them. She could feel it hard against her stomach. "Yes." A needy cry was torn from her lips. She shouldn't do this. It was dangerous. Not just in the physical sense either. It was dangerous for her. Cordia didn't get jealous. These were new emotions. New feelings welled up in her. Feelings she had no business harboring. It felt so good. Too good. She groaned, wanting more.

Stone growled, sounding frustrated and he continued to finger-fuck her. "So damned beautiful," he muttered. Almost to himself. He tore her tank top open, dipping his head down to suck on her nipples. His mouth sent zings of need straight to her core.

By now Cordia was panting hard. Her orgasm, hovering somewhere just below the surface. "What's wrong? I'm ready. Take me, dragon."

He groaned again, his eyes went from desire-filled to pained. "I owe you one, remember? I should…" He dropped to his knees, his eyes between her legs. They zoned in on her snatch.

For an arrogant ass, the male was extremely sweet. She watched as he leaned in, preparing to ease her. "Wait a minute." She cupped his chin. "I want you badly. As in, inside me, and right now."

"But… I can—"

"No buts. I told you that you don't owe me anything and I meant it. You need to know upfront…" Blast, but she was turned on. Her nipples tight little nubs. Her snatch clenched with need. Her clit throbbed. "I can't have any kind of relationship…"

He stood up, covering her mouth with a finger. "We'll discuss it later. We'll argue about it." He grinned. It was sexy and tense with his desire. "I'll enjoy every second of that argument."

"There is nothing to—"

"Shhhh…." He covered her mouth with his. "Not now." He slipped a finger back inside her and she moaned. "I'm feeling really turned on right now. I want you so badly… to be inside you… really deep. I can tell by how wet this pussy is that you want the same. You want to scream my name, Cordia. Don't you dare make me stop."

"You *wish* I would scream your name, dragon." She smiled, sucking in a breath when he rubbed on her clit using his thumb.

She grabbed hold of his cock, giving it a tug. Stone's eyes drifted shut and he made a growling sound that she'd come to recognize as arousal.

Cordia kept her hand around his thick girth, giving him another tug. "Take me already." Feral males were base. They put a female on all fours, got her wet and did the deed. Stone was toying with her and it both excited and frustrated her. Thankfully, the time for games had come to an end.

Stone crouched down a little so that he could position his head at her opening.

"Maybe it would be easier if we did this on the bed or on the floor." She licked her lips. "From behind would be safer."

Stone shook his head. "Fuck being safe." He pushed his tip into her. "The only thing that would concern me is getting you with child, but that's not going to happen."

She wanted to dwell on that remark. Unpack it. Analyze the hell out of it. Maybe confess a couple of things to Stone while she was at it.

The dragon thrust into her. He used a hard, even stroke that took her breath away. That had her forgetting everything but them, and the here and now. This hour, this minute, this second. This was wrong on all levels. He thrust again, using a hard, punchy stroke that had her moaning loudly. She put her hand on either side on the surface under her ass. A high, narrow table.

Stone lifted her knees, making the next thrust hit places she never knew she had. She groaned. He wrapped a hand under her legs, holding her in a tilted-up position. That had her eyes widening and her mouth opening.

Cordia's head rolled back against the wall and she made a whimpering sound. "Feels good," she somehow managed to grind out as he picked up the pace.

He thrust into her again, deeper this time and she cried out.

"You okay?" His eyes were filled with both concern and lust. His jaw was tense, his whole expression told her that he was on edge. His brow was deeply creased. How funny that the dragon was worried about her. He should be concerned about his own safety.

Cordia found it in herself to smile. "I won't break. Fuck me already. I'll try hard not to hurt you!" She yelled the last word as he thrust again. That coiling feeling was already taking hold.

It was all that Stone needed because he began to thrust into her like a male possessed. A deep growl filled the room. Hard and throaty. Giving her everything he had. His eyes were locked with hers. He grunted loudly with every stroke. It was… it was hot. It was intense A sheen of sweat gleamed on his brow. His neck muscles were all over the place.

His prick hit nerve-endings inside her that lit up like gold in the sun. She moaned as his pelvis ground against hers, as his hips rocked with hers. As his breath mingled with hers.

"Come for me, gorgeous." His eyes glowed, while his body demanded more from her. He clenched his jaw and his hands tightened on her.

It was useless to fight it, even though she wanted this moment to last. Wanted him joined with her for longer than one more stolen time. In the end, it was useless to hold back.

Everything in her tightened as she felt herself free-fall. Cordia moaned his name. Stone jerked against her. She could feel his heat erupt inside of her. He groaned her name as he leaned into her neck. As her snatch coupled with him, suctioning onto him, milking him, his eyes opened wide and his mouth opened. He clenched his jaw for a moment and then roared. The male sounded like he was in agony. Even though Cordia was still coming down from her own powerful orgasm, she did a double-check that she wasn't grabbing him or squeezing him. He groaned long and deep, still moving, in round circular motions. Staying deep and connected. He leaned in, nipping at her neck. His teeth felt good. They felt... He bit down. Not hard and yet—

A second, even more powerful orgasm was pulled out of her as Stone clamped down. She could feel her blood rushing through her veins. Cordia sucked in a deep breath and screamed. It felt so good that it almost hurt as her muscles spasmed over and over as wave after wave crashed through her. Stone roared a second time as well, his neck muscles corded and his eyes rolled back.

Thankfully, he released her, slumping over her, his hips still rocking, his prick still deep. Still hard.

Cordia slumped forward against him. She couldn't seem to catch her breath. The table suddenly crashed out from under her. Stone's grip on her tightened. He somehow managed to hold her up. He leaned her up against the wall for a few moments before easing out of her and lowering her down. He kept a grip on her as her legs threatened to buckle. Another first.

His chest heaved against hers. Not nearly as labored for the amount of work, not to mention saving her from falling onto her backside. His whole body vibrated and shook as he began to laugh.

She swallowed hard between desperate pants, trying to hold back a laugh of her own and failed. They both eventually howled with laughter.

"Arghh!" Stone groaned. "I think you might have cracked another rib, or possibly busted my hip." He gripped his side.

"Oh no! Oh..." Cordia felt adrenaline hit her system. "I told you. I warned you." That second roar had been more about pain than pleasure. Her eyes felt huge. "I'm so sorry. You shouldn't have bitten me like that." Worry eased off when she saw how he was grinning. He still clutched his side. There was a light sheen on his brow. She wasn't sure if it was from the exertion or pain.

"I'm still hard." He glanced down at his prick and indeed, it jutted proudly from his body. "My injuries can't be that bad. Besides, they're well worth it. As to the biting…" He shook his head. "Yeah, I probably shouldn't have done that." He made a face.

"I could have killed you."

"Not for that reason." His turned serious. "I shouldn't have done it since it is mating behavior." He frowned deeply, looking like he was thinking it over. "I've never bitten anyone before." He still looked confused. "I had an overwhelming urge to—"

She pulled away as another shot of adrenaline hit her system. What the hell was she doing? Her clothes hung off her in tatters. "You really need to go now."

"I knew that would scare you, but I decided to tell you anyway. Please give us a chance. If the sex scares you, we could back off on the physical aspect…for a while." He chuckled. "My hip might take a day or two to properly heal. I want to get to know you, Cordia."

"No way!"

"Why are you so against this? It was my understanding that the Feral… that your kind are very quick to decide on a mate. You admitted you were jealous. You—"

"I admitted no such thing."

"You blush easily for a big, bad Feral. You didn't need to verbally admit to it. I could see it written all over you. Just like I can see it now. You fucking loved it when I bit you. I doubt you've ever come so hard."

She swallowed thickly. "The sex is good. It means

nothing."

"It means a lot and you know it. Compatibility is one of the cornerstones in a relationship."

"One of them. We don't have anything else." She folded her arms.

"I disagree." That half-smile was back.

"What do you want with a female who will never be able to bear you young?" She clenched her jaw, feeling hurt well up inside her.

His jaw tightened and his eyes darkened. She had struck a nerve. "I said not to think too far into the future."

"That is foolish talk. What happens two years from now, or ten, for that matter, when you are bitter and angry because you are unable to follow your basic drive to procreate? What then? I assure you that you will take it out on me. On us. Even if you don't want to. You won't be able to help yourself."

"I would never." He shook his head vehemently.

"You can't say that!"

"I can and I am."

"Just go!" She didn't mean it. She wanted him to stay. She wanted to have more sex. She wanted to talk. To laugh. To share. Cordia wanted him to stay so badly it scared her senseless.

CHAPTER 10

Stone heard her loud and clear when she told him to leave. It had to be for the fifth or sixth time since he had turned up at her door. He didn't believe that she really wanted him gone. He could see it. Could scent it. Could feel it in his gut.

This female could be the one.

His female.

She felt it too, just as much as he did. Maybe even more so… and yet she was denying it. There was something she wasn't telling him. Something important. He was sure of it. "I would never do that to you. I would never leave because of something you had no control over. For a choice that I made."

She looked down at the ground, looking sad and disappointed. "You believe that now but give it a few years and you would grow to hate me."

"That would never happen." He took her hand, but she

pulled away. "My sister killed herself," he blurted. He had planned on telling her about Amethyst, but not like this. "My twin sister." He swallowed a lump down as it formed in his throat.

Cordia gasped, her eyes filling with concern. She shook her head. "I'm sorry. That's awful."

He nodded. "Yes, it is. It happened a few years back. Our kings had just announced the Hunt. The first one had just taken place. You know about the Hunt, don't you?"

She got a look of distaste and nodded once. "I know enough about it."

Stone nodded once. "My sister's mate left her to try to capture a human. He changed his mind about wanting to have children. It is as you said. He slowly grew bitter about not being able to ever be a father. They grew apart."

A tear rolled down Cordia's cheek. It tore him up to see her upset. She swiped it away, eyes blazing with anger. "I hope you killed him!"

Stone shook his head. "No. I couldn't. I wanted to but... I couldn't in the end. The male was distraught. I have never seen someone grieve like that. He never ended up going on even a single Hunt. Hasn't so much as looked at another female since. He has punished himself."

Stone raked a hand through his hair. "You are right. We are driven. He thought that having kids was what he wanted, that it was worth anything, even giving up the female he loved, but he was dead wrong. Amethyst was everything to him and he threw it away. I would never hurt a female in the same way." He grit his teeth. "I wouldn't. I know that for a fact. I know that if Druze could do things over, he would make very different decisions. I have learned from his mistake."

She nodded once, her mind working.

What was going through her mind?

"I had a sister once," she whispered. "I lost her too. I understand your pain."

"I'm sorry. It's terrible when someone is taken too soon. I believe that Amethyst died from a broken heart, even though she took her own life. She lost her mate. She blamed herself. Her infertility." Stone took her hand. "So, if that's your only concern, you can set it aside. Unless there's something else?" He looked at her, giving her an opening if there was something on her mind. At the same time, trying not to be too forceful. This thing was moving fast. Probably too fast but... it felt right somehow. This was right. *They* were right! "Is there something else holding you back, Cordia?" he tried again.

Her eyes flared with sudden panic. The moment gone almost immediately. *Shit!* There was definitely something else, but she wasn't going to tell him what that something was. "I think we should stick to the original plan and not think too far ahead. I think we need a quick shower." She smiled as she stepped forward, slipping her hands around his neck. "I think we can work on getting dirtier before we get clean... unless," she frowned, "you're not feeling up to it."

Cordia was using sex to duck out of telling him her real fears about a potential relationship. He'd take it. It was better than having her kick him out. He squeezed his hip. "I'm damaged but not broken." Then he grinned, leaning down to capture her lips. Full and beautiful. Cordia moaned, so wonderfully receptive. He pulled back, nipping at her lower lip as he did. "We might need to take it easy. We definitely need to be more careful."

"I told you." She narrowed her eyes. "Our species are not as compatible as you think."

"Shhhh." He kissed her again to shut her up. "Not true at all. We broke another table, didn't we?"

"I'm heavy."

"More like, we're explosive together." Stone stepped out of his pants, which were still snagged around his ankles. "Let's get in the shower and then I'm getting into you."

Another flare of something in her eyes. Something... it was gone. Cordia nodded once and turned in the direction of the bathroom. She'd open up to him soon enough. He winced as he took the first step. She'd wrapped her legs around him and had squeezed the crap out of him when she'd come for the second time. Stone was sure he had heard a crack. It had been worth it to see her come so hard. He was already on the mend. Sex aided healing. Cordia pulled her own clothing off as she walked ahead of him.

Her ass was a piece of art. Perky and tight. Her legs. *Fuck!* They went on for miles. Even her long, elegant back was sexy. All of it encased in smooth silky skin he was dying to get his hands on all over again.

She opened the shower door and leaned in, turning on the faucet. Cordia threw him an almost shy smile from under her lashes as she stepped under the water. She turned, water dripping down her body. Soaking her black hair. Running over her perky little tits. They reminded him of ripe peaches. The smaller tastier kind. Dark plump nipples had his mouth salivating.

With a low growl, he stepped into the stall with her, closing the door behind them. "We don't have too much time." He gripped her hip.

She got a look he couldn't put his finger on. Like she was hurt. Why did saying what he had hurt her? Before he had a chance to analyze her reaction, her eyes became hooded and she bit down on her lower lip.

"Turn around." He kept his eyes on her gorgeous honeyed irises as he spoke.

He half expected her to argue but she did as he asked. Stone's cock was hard. His balls tight. They tightened even more with anticipation as he watched her move into position. He couldn't wait to get inside her again.

"Open up for me." He stuck his knee between her thighs.

Cordia moaned, she glanced back over her shoulder. "You've become demanding all of a sudden."

He palmed her ass. Moving closer, so that his hard cock was against her. "You drive me insane." He slipped his fingers over her slit. "Fuck, you're wet." This female was so damned receptive. It was a highly prized quality in any female. She did drive him insane, but she also brought out every base instinct in him. Ones that told him to take, to mate. It did scare him some. He had never expected feelings like this. Then to have them develop so suddenly… Stone would need to hold back a whole lot. Otherwise he was going to scare her off. He rubbed ever so softly on her clit.

She laughed. It held a melodic quality. Like she was singing. "Of course, I'm wet," she moaned. "We're in the shower." The gorgeous female stuck her ass out further, arching her back. She was just as desperate for this as he was. Her body made tiny circular motions against his fingers, clearly wanting more.

Stone dipped two fingers inside her. "You're wet in every which way."

She tilted her head back. "Mount me already, dragon." Her voice had a desperate edge that he loved.

"So damned impatient. Haven't you ever heard of foreplay?"

"Sure… but I'm wet. That is what foreplay is about isn't it?"

"Not on your life, Feral, and if we had more time, I would prove it to you. I still plan on eating your pussy again. I don't think I've ever tasted anything quite so exquisite. I want you to come on my face again."

Her breathing turned ragged, he eased up, not wanting her to come just yet. Her scent grew even sweeter, even more tempting. "That sounds good." Her words were rushed and breathy. "Right now, I want your prick… inside me."

The stream from the shower pelted his back. "Your wish is my command." Stone moved between her thighs and thrust into her tight confines, hitting home immediately. He snarled at how fucking amazing she felt. He began to move. His breath turned ragged in an instant. She had such a snug pussy. He had to squeeze his eyes shut to keep from shooting off. It was like she hadn't had sex in a good long while. That's how fucking gloriously tight she was. It couldn't be though. Not a beauty like Cordia. She must have males lining up to be with her. Not something he wanted to think about just then. It made him feel… jealous. Definitely not going there in that moment.

He drove deeper into her tight heat. Sex had never been this good before. Not ever. He knew he was attracted to her and that they would be compatible, but this was next-level stuff. His gums ached and his scales rubbed. His dragon wanted him to mate her. It wanted him to vocally claim her and demanded that she do the same back. It wanted him to bite her again. This time it wanted him to mark her as well. Stone hadn't been lying when he'd told her he'd never experienced this before.

He pressed his body against hers, not giving her much room to move. More mating behavior. Hold a female down. Keep her immobile. Then take, take, take and mark. Her fingers were splayed on the glass. They made little slipping noises. Her breasts would be pressed against the side of the stall as well. A sight that would be something to behold, he was sure. She panted and groaned and moaned and whimpered. Each and every sound drove him more and more crazy with need. What was it about her that made him feel more like an animal than a rational, level-headed person?

Stone continued to pound into her. He loved that suctioning feeling around him. It told him she was close. He knew what was to come. How much more intense this would become. He fucking loved the noises their bodies made as they came together. The slapping of his balls. The thudding sound as his hips hit her ass. The wet noises as his cock slid in and out of her wet pussy. He could hear it all above the pouring water cascading down his back.

Stone bent his knee, wanting to—Cordia cried out. *Yeah, right there.* Her pussy began to flutter around his dick. It began to suction, just a little. He grunted hard with each thrust, as pleasure pulled his balls tight, working to keep from coming. *Not yet!* Even the noises he was making were odd to him; he normally rutted in silence. Aside from heavy breathing, he normally kept really quiet. All this grunting and roaring was new. Probably more mating behavior. That, or it was how good she felt. Probably a combination of both. With another loud grunt, he palmed her breasts. Her mammary glands were amazing. Soft. Her nipples were dark and ripe. They were plump and tightened with just a glance. He squeezed her flesh, enjoying how she felt against his palms. His hands slipped and slid over her wet flesh.

Cordia shouted his name, her pussy clamped down around him. His balls pulled up all the way. His skin tightened. The air froze in his lungs. The inside of her pussy suctioned onto the tip of his cock.

He pulled in a hard breath and his eyes widened. The sensation surprised him all over again, even though he'd felt this twice before. He lifted his head and roared as he lost his load in hard spurts that almost hurt. He kept his hands clamped on her hips and jerked into her. Cordia gave a loud yell as her suctioning pussy began to spasm. Stone couldn't help himself, he had to sink his teeth into her. Just a careful nip. Just a—He growled as his teeth bore down.

Cordia screamed his name, her whole body seemed to spasm around him even harder. Every muscle tensed for the longest time. He squeezed her breasts and rolled her nipples between his fingers, loving how good she felt. How right this felt.

Using easy circular thrusts, he wrung out the last of her pleasure, as well as his own, already dreading pulling out of her. This level of need was not normal.

"You shouldn't have done that." She sounded angry. Now that he was thinking about it, he realized how tense she felt. How rigid the line of her back was. Thankfully the suctioning began to let up.

Stone pulled out, noticing that he had almost broken the skin on her neck. *Holy fuck!* He needed to be careful. This could get out of hand. "I'm sorry. You enjoyed it so I…" *Gave in to my instincts.* He couldn't say that because it would scare her even more.

"It's mating behavior." She turned around, eyes hard and narrowed. "And it's not going to happen between us. You and I are not going to happen. The sex has been good, but this is over."

Stone watched her walk out of the bathroom, towel in hand. He followed, watching as she grabbed clothing from her closet, getting dressed while still damp. He wanted to try to change her mind, but he could see it would be a losing battle right then. She was too pissed at him. She also looked… afraid. There was something more going on. Why was she afraid? There had to be something. Probably something important. Instead of saying what was on his mind, he toweled off and picked up his pants, putting them on.

"I'll see you at lunch then?" He sounded hopeful. He sounded damned pathetic, but it couldn't be helped.

Cordia nodded once, looking anywhere but at him.

That was a resounding 'no' if he ever saw one. "Okay then. For what it's worth, I'm sorry. I shouldn't have bitten you again." He shook his head.

"You shouldn't have bitten me at all." She pulled in a deep breath. "Look, what's done is done. You didn't actually mate me."

"There is more involved for that to happen. I would never go that far. I swear." He held up both hands.

Cordia nodded again, her face unreadable. "You still

went too far and you're pushing too hard." Then she folded her arms and glanced at the door.

Stone could take a hint. Especially if said hint wasn't so subtle. "I need to change, so I'll get going. I'll see you in ten." Pathetic! He couldn't help but hope that she showed up.

Another nod. Her features were grim. He wished he knew what was going on inside her head. Walking out was hard. Only because he wanted to push her for answers. She was feeling this pull between them. It scared her for some reason. It scared him too but not like her. It scared him in a way that made him want to talk. Cordia was completely closed off. Worse still, she was running. There was something she was hiding. He knew it just as sure as he knew his own name.

CHAPTER 11

S tone pushed his plate away, half his steak uneaten. The food sat in his stomach like a rock.

"You okay?" Topaz asked, frowning. "You're awfully broody for a male who just got lucky."

"Sex isn't everything," he muttered, looking around the dining hall. Delfinia was pushing her chair back, preparing to leave. She was the last of the group still there. Aside from him and Topaz. He checked the clock on the wall. Five minutes before their afternoon session began. Still no sign of Cordia. He sat there for almost an hour, eyes on the door, hoping she would turn up. Knowing full well it wasn't going to happen.

"What? Did you knock your head as well? I happened to notice the limp when you walked in earlier." She snort-laughed. "Your head looks fine to me though." She pretended to scrutinize his skull. "I don't think I've ever heard a male say that before. Sex normally ranks way up there. Are you sure you didn't knock your head while you were getting it on? And don't try to deny it. I can scent it from a mile away."

"Funny haha. You're a laugh a minute. I wouldn't try to deny it," he grumbled.

"Definitely in a bad mood, which, again... doesn't compute. Was it bad or something?"

"Was what bad?" He took a sip of his water.

"The sex." She kept her voice down even though they were alone. "I thought you two had chemistry. At least, I assumed it, based on the broken table and the events that have unfolded since."

He shrugged. "I thought so too."

"Oh," she smiled, looking sorry for him at the same time, "Cordia doesn't feel the same? Was the sex good for you but not so great for her? Maybe we aren't compatible as species."

"We are!" he snapped back.

"Okay, okay." She held up a hand. "Touchy. So, the sex was amazing. That's not the issue. So... what's the problem then?" She frowned.

"I have no idea. I'm stumped. She's into me... I know she is, but she's pushing me away. Why? Like you said, the sex is fucking amazing. She's amazing. *We* could be amazing."

Topaz dropped her fork on the table with a clunk. "You have feelings for her." Her mouth fell open. Then she choked out a laugh. "Oh my god! I can't believe it. You are crushing on a Feral."

"Crushing? What kind of talk is that? Non-humans don't have crushes. We fuck or we mate, there is rarely an in-between."

Topaz slapped a hand over her mouth, her eyes were bright and filled with excitement. "You want to mate her." She spoke through her fingers before removing her hand. "It's serious then?"

"It's too soon to be talking about mating, but I'm serious about her. I want more. I want to get to know this female. I want to spend time with her. I want her to come back to my lair. I want to get to know her people, her life. I—"

"By freaking scale… you're in love."

"I don't know Cordia well enough to say that… yet."

"Yet?" She raised her brows.

He gave a one-shouldered shrug. "I don't think it would take much to fall for her."

Topaz giggled. "I knew it. This is so romantic. You guys have been at each other's throats the entire time – well almost the entire time – and now…" She bit down on her bottom lip. "You're an 'enemies to lovers' romance. It doesn't get much better."

"We're hardly enemies and we're… definitely not lovers." He sighed. "That's the problem. She still hates me."

"She does *not* hate you. I've seen the looks she gives you and trust me, I don't see a single shred of hate there." Topaz frowned, looking concerned. "You do know that she more than likely can't have children. She wouldn't be here otherwise. We were all picked to attend to represent our species for a reason. You, because of what happened to your sister. You know first-hand how this crisis is affecting our females… our whole community, for that matter."

"I don't care if she's infertile. It isn't important to me."

Stone had always wanted young. He'd always seen himself as a future father. Would he be disappointed if it never happened? Yes. Absolutely. Did it deter him? *Fuck no!* "She can't have young, but I want to get to know her anyway."

"You really do have it bad. You—"

Just then, the door opened, and Gazelle stuck her head around the jamb, she was smiling but looked tense. "Oh good. There you are." Her smile suddenly looked forced.

"We were just about to head to the conference room," Topaz said. They both pushed their chairs back.

"Great! You go on through, Topaz." She turned to him. "There is something I need to discuss with you, Stone."

"Oh… okay." Topaz nodded, she looked his way, widening her eyes for a second or two in question. "I'll see you there," she said to him and then headed out.

"Close the door behind you?" Gazelle asked.

Oh shit! What now? Had Helga or Lexi stirred up more trouble? "Whatever they said, don't believe them," he blurted.

Gazelle narrowed her eyes, frowning. "I'm not sure what you mean."

Crap! He was wrong then. It wasn't the vampire and the wolf. "What's up?" He tried to lean back in his chair and to play it cool, yet somehow, he had a feeling he wasn't going to like what the vampire had to say.

She looked tense. Gazelle kept clasping and unclasping her hands. She'd licked her lips three times already since entering the room and couldn't hold his gaze for longer than a second or two. "It's Cordia." She looked down at her lap.

"What about her?"

"She came to see me during the lunch break."

"Yeah?" he finally prompted when the vampire didn't go on of her own accord.

"I'm not quite sure how to say this." More clasping and unclasping of her hands. More licking of her lips.

"Just say it. Lay it on me." *Yep!* Looked like he had been right. He was going to hate this.

"She says that," she winced, "you are stalking her." She spoke quickly. Like if she got it out quicker, it wouldn't sound as bad as it did. No such luck!

"What?" he practically yelled.

"I'm sorry. Please don't shoot the messenger. She says you won't leave her alone. You won't leave when she asks you to. In fact, you barged your way into her apartment earlier after she insisted you leave."

"We had a disagreement which needed hashing out, so no, I wouldn't leave until we had talked things through. She was being unreasonable." He bit down on his tongue, realizing how stalkerish he sounded right then.

Gazelle's stance didn't change. This time she looked him in the eyes. "She said that you insisted on having," she cleared her throat, "sex…"

"What? You can't be serious! It was completely consensual. We—"

"She didn't dispute that it was consensual. She said it was just rutting to her, but that you have developed an unhealthy infatuation with her. Cordia made it clear that she doesn't want any more contact with you. She wants you to stop stalking her… sorry," she held up a hand, "her words, not mine."

What the fuck?! "I'm not…" he began. "I'm not stalking Cordia. I—"

"Look," Gazelle interrupted him. Her voice was soothing. She looked at him with pity. "I'm not sure what's going on between the two of you. It's clear to me that it's two-sided. Not just coming from you. I don't want to know any of the details. Quite frankly it's none of my business. What I do know is that a complaint was laid. She asked that it remain unofficial as long as you stay away. She has asked to be given another partner. I'm going to pair you with Penelope. Cordia will partner with Bonnie. I strongly suggest you stay far away from the Feral. Don't strike up a conversation. Don't go to her after hours. Don't so much as sit next to her. Stay far away from her, please. I don't want this officially reported. There'll be an inquiry. You could get me into trouble as well." Her eyes were wide. "This could put this entire conference at risk. Not just this one in particular, but for future forums. We have more planned but on a much greater scale. This one was preliminary, a beta, if you will, to see what measures need to be implemented. I can certainly think of one or two." She realized she'd digressed. "I can't have this turning into an issue. Please!"

"I understand," he pushed out the word, sounding defeated. He should be angry. Spitting mad! Instead, he felt disappointed and worried. What was going on with Cordia? What had spooked her so badly that she felt the need to take such drastic measures? Screw inquiries. Screw getting into trouble. Their issues were not going to affect this or any future events. Stone was getting to the bottom of this. Cordia was going to damn well tell him what was going on with her.

Cordia's face felt hot. She burned with shame. She'd panicked. She'd been forced to find a way to get Stone off her back. To make him stop pushing for a relationship. For more between them. She'd panicked and had gone to see Gazelle. She'd blurted out the first thing that came to mind. Thing was, she had to ensure that she was taken seriously by the female. Gazelle had been clear that swapping partners was not permitted. So, her excuse had to be good.

Stone was stalking her.

Stalking.

Her.

Her cheeks heated some more. Maybe she shouldn't have said such a thing. It was a horrible accusation. Especially when it wasn't true. *No!* It was the right thing to have done. She didn't trust herself around the male. Cordia had been jealous. She loved hearing him say that he liked her. That there was something real between them. She loved that he wanted to spend time with her… getting to know her in all ways. Not just physical. He wasn't even put off by her fertility problems. He was a good male. Caring, sweet, funny and sexy. Cordia wanted to know more about him.

The story about his sister had rocked her to her core. Then there was the sex. It was… it was surreal. All of it was. Cordia loved how he made her feel. Like she was the only female on the planet. Like she was all he would ever need. Hence the panic that had set in. Especially when he'd bitten her. It had all felt so right. Like a puzzle piece falling into place. This spark, this thing, given just the tiniest bit of kindling and it would flame. Before long, it would be a raging inferno. That was why she had forced herself to do what she had done. She'd smothered that spark before anything more could come of it.

The door opened and closed. It was the last delegate. It was Stone. She didn't want to look at him. He'd be angry. Maybe he even hated her now. She wouldn't blame him. She wouldn't be able to take it though. To see the hate shining in his eyes. His beautiful eyes. Maybe he'd mount Helga or Lexi. Or both. Probably both. He'd do it to spite her. She couldn't blame him for that either. She'd deserve it. Cordia needed to stick to her plan though. She needed to protect herself. For that matter, she needed to protect them both.

She heard him sit down. Just like on the first day, it was across the table from her, only this time, it was a little to the left instead of directly across from her.

Cordia kept her eyes on the paper in front of her, pretending to scan it. She had been taking reading lessons online. Most of the Feral had. She'd picked it up easily. They were a species who adapted easily. She didn't read the page though. She couldn't. The top of her head prickled too badly.

Blast and damn! She could feel him looking at her. His eyes burning holes in her. Maybe she should apologize. Take it back. Set the record straight.

No!

Forget it. She'd done the right thing. She needed to stick to the plan. Keep the male at arm's length until she got back to her own territory. Then she needed to forget all about him. The last would be tough but she was sure she could do it. They weren't in too deep yet. Besides, he hated her now, so it would make things easier. She pushed out a slow breath. She had done the right thing. She had!

A female cleared her throat at the head of the table. It was Gazelle. "Welcome back. There has been a small change to the teams." The female paused for a moment. "Cordia and Stone are no longer partners."

Helga gasped and Lexi giggled. One or two of the others reacted as well. "Stone is now paired with Bonnie and Penelope with Cordia. Thank you to all parties for agreeing to the change."

"Why though?" Helga asked.

"It is not relevant to these proceedings," Gazelle said. "Now if—"

"I thought we couldn't swap." The female shook her head, looking amused.

"You can't."

"But—" the vampire began.

"Moving on," Gazelle said in a firm voice.

Cordia saw Helga's smug grin as the female turned to look at her. She ignored the vampire bitch, praying Stone didn't seek vengeance by mounting someone like that.

Please!

"We are going to discuss interspecies relationships this afternoon." Gazelle cleared her throat, looking distinctly uncomfortable. "The advantages and the pitfalls. Let's start with the pitfalls. I'll write them down on the board. Who would like to begin?"

Cordia glanced at Stone. She had hoped that his attention would be on Gazelle. It wasn't. Her heart sped up. He was staring at her.

Feathers and tar.

The male didn't look angry. He held her gaze, lifting a brow in question. He looked slightly amused. Not put out at all.

Feathers and tar in a hailstorm. He wasn't deterred. Not in the slightest.

"Does anyone have any pitfalls they can think of?" Gazelle tried again.

"Cultural differences could make it impossible," Cordia said, trying hard to take her eyes off of his.

Stone winked at her. Her heart practically leapt out of his chest. He gave her this sexy half-smile. "I disagree," Stone announced, sitting up taller in his seat, his gaze turning to Gazelle. "I think differences should be embraced and nurtured. Communication is key. Some species prefer not to communicate. It's a mistake." He glanced her way as he finished.

"Sometimes differences are so vast that no amount of communication will help." Cordia countered, also looking at Gazelle. "It would be a futile exercise, so why bother?"

"It may not be futile. That's the thing. It may—"

"Does anyone else have anything to offer?" Gazelle asked, sounding tense.

Sweet Delfinia put her hand up and Gazelle visibly relaxed. "I think that…" the elf began.

It looked like she had only made him more determined. Why the hell was she feeling so excited about the prospect? It was wrong on every level. It was stupid. It was rash. She should leave at once. She should get up and leave. Not just the room but vampire territory as well. She should rush home with her tail firmly between her legs.

Cordia was there on important business. All-important. Her best friend was depending on her. Cordia was a strong female. A Feral. She could keep her distance from the male despite his obvious plans to the contrary. Her heart sped up. Thrumming in her chest.

CHAPTER 12

S he heard footfalls behind her. "Cordia. Wait. I wanted to talk to you."

Arghhh! She lifted her eyes to the sky for a moment, contemplating ignoring the female. For a moment there, she had been so sure that she had slipped away unnoticed.

Surora arrived a few seconds later, slightly out of breath. "I'm glad I caught you," she said.

"Let's walk and talk," Cordia countered, picking up the pace again. "It's been a long day and I'm tired." Sitting across from Stone had been taxing. She couldn't take anymore. Once she got to her nest, she'd be home-free.

Cordia snuck a peek over her shoulder. *Oh, thank the gods!* He wasn't following her. She let out a sigh of relief but kept on walking just in case.

"You're worried he's following, aren't you?"

"I don't know what you're talking about," she mumbled, hoping that Surora would drop it. It wasn't a conversation she wanted to have with the female. With anyone, for that matter.

"You know exactly what I'm referring to," Surora shot back. "The male, Stone. I don't need developed senses to tell that there is a whole lot going on between the two of you."

"There is nothing going on."

"That's why you asked to swap partners."

"How do you know it had anything to do with me? Any of the four of us could have requested the swap, yet you automatically assume it was me." She touched her chest.

"It was definitely you, Cordia. Why deny it?"

Cordia kept walking. She finally arrived at her nest, taking another look around them. "I don't wish to talk about it. It's not important."

"It is if you asked to swap partners. Don't try to deny it was you. Penelope and Bonnie were both shocked. You didn't so much as flinch. You knew it was going to happen. I think you like the dragon. It's the first time I've seen you give a male more than a cursory glance. Yet, you are distancing yourself from him."

"I distance myself from all males. Not that our males have much interest in me."

"You close yourself off from our males."

Cordia frowned. "It's more than that and you know it."

"You are right, to a degree. Back to the dragon. You look at him in a way I've never seen you look at anyone before."

"Stay out of it. It's none of your business. Now if you'll excuse—"

"You haven't told him, have you?" Surora lifted her brows.

"We had sex. That was it. There is nothing to tell him."

"I understand why you're afraid to—"

"You don't understand anything!" Cordia retaliated – and more fiercely than she'd intended. Surora was only trying to help. She meant well.

The female flinched. "You're right. I don't understand, but I can imagine. I know I'm interfering and that it's none of my business, but you should talk to him. If you like him – I mean really like him – then you should, at least, be honest. You never know—"

"I do know! It wouldn't help anything." She shook her head. "I don't want to talk about it anymore. As I said, I'm tired and—"

"And you need to get ready for our dinner?" The other female's eyes lit up. "Do you have an outfit?"

They had all been invited to a formal sit-down dinner, as this was their last evening together. Cordia shook her head. She could think of nothing worse. To sit and mingle while trying hard to avoid Stone. "I'm not going," she suddenly decided.

Surora's mouth fell open. "It's compulsory. You have to go."

"I don't feel up to it." She shook her head again.

"You should come this evening and you should talk to Stone. Your eyes get all… weird when he is close. Did you know that?"

"There is nothing for him and me to talk about." She ignored the comment about her eyes lighting up. "Things are the way they are. I have no place in my life for Stone or any male. It doesn't matter what I want. Or need. It is a simple fact. I will excuse myself tonight. I know that Gazelle will understand."

"It must be awful! I thought being infertile was bad. That it was a terrible fate, but I was wrong, wasn't I? The alternative is worse."

"Yes, I'm afraid it's true."

Surora reached out and clasped her hand. She gave it a squeeze.

"Thank you," Cordia said, nodding once. "I appreciate… that you wanted to help."

"If you change your mind about this evening, I have a dress you could wear. I would be happy to sit next to you."

"I won't change my mind." She shook her head.

"I know. I thought I would try anyway."

Stone arrived ten minutes late. He was nervous. Sweaty palms and all. Nervous she wouldn't be there and even more nervous that she would. His heart sank as he walked through the door. He walked inside, looking around the room. Stone did a second sweep of the room. Cordia liked being on time. She took things seriously. Why wasn't she there then?

It was him.

He had pushed too hard.

Stalked her.

Fuck!

Helga's face lit up as she looked his way. She wore a bright red gown with a plunging neckline. She smiled at him. *Double cluster fuck!* How did he get out of this one? Just then, his pocket began to vibrate. *Saved by the bell.*

Stone pulled his phone out of his pocket and answered, spinning away from the female to make himself very clear. "Hello," he said without even looking to see who had been calling. He didn't care. Anyone was better than trying to get Helga off his back. The female was infuriating with her advances. Any more forward and it could be deemed... stalking.

Fuck!

Was he Helga in reverse? *Maybe. No! Fuck... maybe.* "Hey, are you there? Can you hear me? Is the signal bad, bud?" It was Sand. Stone wasn't sure how long the male had been talking to him.

"Yes. I can hear you," he quickly blurted.

"Oh good! How are you doing? I'm not interrupting, am I? I can hear you're not alone. Are you still in talks?"

"No. Nothing like that. We're having dinner for our final night... or about to... and I'm... good, you?" He pushed a breath out.

"Fucking amazing," his friend gushed. "I've never been happier. Well, I'm also worried... very fucking worried, but I'm mainly stoked as hell."

"Good. Glad to hear it You might need to explain about the worried part though. Is everything okay?" Stone frowned.

"Mace is pregnant, buddy. She's with child... my children. I'm going to be a father. Fuck! I've never been happier. She's over the moon. So fucking happy." He chuckled. "We both are."

His eyes widened. "That's brilliant news, bro!" Stone shouted, attracting everyone's attention. He smiled, making his way out of the room. "Why the worry then? Enjoy it! It's such fantastic news. How's Mace? She must be thrilled."

"That's just it." Sand went from upbeat to down in an instant. "She's been really sick. Throwing up once or twice a day."

"That's normal, isn't it?"

"Yes, I know." Sand pushed out a solid breath. "It all makes me quite nervous now that she is with child. I don't like seeing her hurting in any kind of way. I can tell I'm going to be one of those raging males who's over-protective. She's not going to like it."

He chuckled. "No, she won't."

"She's also had some pains in her belly which is also supposed to be normal in early pregnancy. Things are stretching inside her… I don't know all the medical lingo. I need to read some of the pregnancy books she has lying around, so I know what to expect." Stone could hear that the male was beaming. "I don't want to keep you. I just wanted to tell you the good news, since you've been there every step of the way."

"Congrats, Sand! Please send Macy my love."

His friend growled.

"I didn't mean it like that, asshole." Stone choked out a laugh.

"Sorry! I know," Sand said. "Back to the part where I'm possessive as fuck."

"You should dig out that present I got you guys. Is it still in the back of your closet?"

"No!" Sand practically shouted. "Not going there yet."

"What? Why?" Stone frowned. "You guys are going to need—"

"Bad luck! It's still early days." His friend sounded so nervous it was almost comical. *Poor male!*

"Early days, my ass. Your female and children will be just fine."

"I would prefer not to take any chances. You'll see what I mean, bro. One of these days, you'll be in my shoes. You'll be worried about a female. *Your* female. So worried you can't think of anything else."

"We'll have to see," Stone mumbled.

"It'll happen for you. Wait and see. Anyway, take care. We'll see you soon."

"Yep… see you soon." He ended the call. Thing was, Stone was worried *now*. There was something wrong with Cordia. Something important. Something she wasn't telling him.

"Dinner will be served in a few minutes," Gazelle announced almost as he walked back into the hall. "We should make our way to the tables shortly," she added.

Stone's heart sank. One quick scan of the room told him that Cordia still hadn't arrived yet. Chances were good she wasn't going to come at all. For a while there, he had hoped she was running late, but it was becoming clearer by the second that such a simple explanation was not likely.

All he wanted to do was to put down the glass of wine he had been nursing for the last hour and head to her apartment. Pursuing Cordia after being accused of stalking her would be too much like… stalking her. Despite the worry that coursed through him, he was beginning to doubt himself. Maybe she really did think he was stalking her. Maybe he had read into things too much. Perhaps the jealousy had been based on sex and nothing more. Cordia had been aloof all afternoon. She had not been afraid to hold his gaze, or to debate certain sticking points when it came to interspecies relationships. She had seemed cold and distant. Fuck, but it all made him want her more.

Maybe he *was* a stalker.

Maybe she was right to have swapped partners and to be staying away.

"She told me she isn't coming." Surora interrupted his thoughts. "I'm sorry, I can't help but notice how you keep glancing at the door. I know you like her. I don't know what's up between the two of you but," she waved her hand, "never mind... I don't want to get mixed up in the whole thing."

"You know whatever it is that's bugging her?" He heard the animation in his voice.

Surora shook her head. "I... um... it... I... I can't tell you anything. Not that there's anything to tell," she quickly added.

"So, there is something!" *Thank fuck!* Stone grinned. Couldn't help himself. It meant he wasn't losing his mind. He wasn't wrong about Cordia. There was something holding her back.

"I didn't say that."

"You didn't have to."

"No, I quite clearly said that there was nothing to tell," Surora shot back.

"Which is code for *there is* something to tell." He bobbed his brows.

"No, it doesn't mean that at all." Surora sounded panicked, which was great. It meant he was on the right track.

"Of course it does. Thanks! I appreciate the heads-up."

"I didn't give you a heads-up. Don't say that!" She widened her eyes.

"You did too. You're a gem."

"Now I understand why you drive Cordia crazy," she huffed, eyes narrowed on him.

"It's my good looks, helped along by this custom-made tux." He smoothed a hand down the lapel of his jacket.

Surora made a noise of frustration. "I don't mean that kind of crazy. I meant the bad kind."

"Of course you meant it like that." He winked. "Thank you." He put the glass down. "Now if you'll excuse me… I feel a terrible headache coming on. I think I'll go and lie down."

Her mouth fell open. "You're going to see her, aren't you?" she whispered. "You do not have anything wrong with you."

"Sure I do. My head hurts something fierce." He put his fingers to his temples for a few moments and then smiled at Surora. "Now, if you'll excuse me…?"

Surora rolled her eyes. "Please don't tell her I said anything. She'll rip my wings off. Maybe even my legs as well."

"I won't tell her." Was it wrong that his heart beat faster hearing how capable of violence she was?

"So, you admit you're going to see her?" She put her hands on her hips, looking both put out and amused.

"Shhhhh." He held a finger to his lips. "Don't say anything to anyone."

"I won't if you won't."

"Fine." He grinned.

"Dragon…" she continued, and he turned back to her. "There is something she's not telling you and it's important. All-important."

"I know. Thank you again." He nodded once as he headed out, filled with resolve.

CHAPTER 13

Cordia stared at the square device mounted on the wall. The one where humans play-acted. In this particular production, several males and one female were robbing some sort of facility. They were intent on stealing a large diamond. Cordia couldn't understand why anyone would go to so much effort for what was essentially a rock. Sure, it was pretty, but worth all that? No way!

It was mildly entertaining at best. She yawned, pushing the button to change to a different acting scenario. *Arghhhh!* It was people pretending to be in love with each other. They were kissing. Then the male was pulling her shirt off. Cordia pushed the button again. Why would people want to watch other people play-act at mounting? It was stupid. It made absolutely no sense.

The next program was boring too. She could shut the device off, but then she'd be in complete silence. All alone. She should be used to it by now. Cordia didn't want to attend the dinner, but she also didn't want to be stuck between these four walls. She couldn't go home either.

Cordia wondered how Vicky was doing, and on a whim, she picked up her phone and dialed her friend. The Feral were no longer off the grid like they had been a year ago. They still had plenty to learn but were making great inroads to catch up with society. They had cellphone towers and were connected to the internet.

Finally, Vicky's voice came on the line, telling Cordia that she wasn't available and to try again later.

Cordia tried again immediately. The same message sounded. She tossed her phone on the bed next to her and slumped back down on the pillows. She hated all this self-pity. It didn't help anything. Maybe she should shift and head out for a flight. Her feathers rubbed beneath her skin. Cordia felt restless and irritable. She couldn't bear lying there for a second longer. Her phone buzzed with an incoming message.

I'm in heat. With Talon. Very busy and very excited. Chat in a few days.

P.S. Everything is going to be okay. I just know it.

No! She was too late. Vicky would be with clutch soon. She might end up with the sickness. Her feathers rubbed harder. Decision made, she climbed off the bed and pulled off the clothes she was wearing, dropping them on the floor at her feet. Then she stepped outside, sucking in a deep breath and preparing to shift. Her eyes were already on the sky above. The stars twinkled. Yes, a good, hard flight was exactly what she needed to get rid of some of this wayward energy.

"Now that's just the kind of greeting I was hoping for." Stone sauntered towards her. He wore a tuxedo. Cordia swallowed hard. She'd read about them when looking for eveningwear attire. Although she preferred him in less. Who was she kidding? In nothing at all. He looked amazing in the suit. It fit him perfectly. From how the pants tapered, to the way the jacket fit across his broad chest. The black fabric brought out the deep purple of his eyes.

By feather, she was forgetting herself. "What are you doing here?" She tried to sound hard and cold, but it came out as a whisper. This male did things to her. Her heart beat out of her chest. She panicked at how the sight of him made her feel better. Safe. Made things a little easier to deal with. Her past, her future. Not just her. Vicky too. Her feelings didn't change things. They were the way they were.

"I came to talk to you." He looked resolute.

She narrowed her eyes. "You're supposed to stay away. You're not allowed—"

"That's all a bunch of bullshit and you know it." He folded his arms. "I'm not stalking you, or forcing you to have sex with me, or any of that other crap."

"Why can't you listen to me, Stone? The reason I went to Gazelle was because you weren't listening in the first place. I don't want anything more to do with you. The sex was great, but it's over." Part of her wanted him to turn around and to go. The bigger part wanted him to stay. Fear bubbled up. It was never going to work between them. This needed to stop. He would never understand.

"I don't get that, Cordia," Stone countered. "You *do* have feelings for me. I know it, so don't try to deny it. We're too good together."

"It's just sex."

"That's bull."

"All I know is that I'm leaving tomorrow and that there can never be anything between us, so there is no point in discussing anything or letting you mount me again."

"You're afraid that if we spend more time together, you'll fall for me more than you have already." He leaned against the wall and rubbed his chin, the stubble catching.

Her mouth quite literally fell open. "You're so arrogant. Please leave me alone. I'm not going to be nice about it anymore. I'm going to—"

"Going to what?" He began advancing. "Report me? Get me into trouble with the vampires? My kings?"

"Yes." She nodded hard.

"Here's the thing – I don't care! They can slap my wrists. Throw me in a cage. They can do whatever they want to me. I won't give up until you tell me that you don't feel anything for me. That you don't think there's anything happening here." He waved a hand between them. "I want you to say the words. I want to hear you deny it."

"I don't have to tell you anything." She sounded frustrated. "You can't do that. Just let this go, I beg you."

He shook his head. *No, he wasn't giving up.* She could see it written all over him. "What's that? You don't *have* to tell me you don't feel anything for me, or you don't *want* to?" There wasn't much space left between them. "I think you don't want to."

"It doesn't matter!"

"Say the words, Cordia, or tell me what's really going on." He reached out and gripped her hand. "I need to know what's happening here. What's going through your mind. I can't give up on what might be between us unless I know the truth." He smiled at her. "I'm afraid I *will* stalk you until I have an answer."

"You wouldn't!"

"I will. You're the one who started this whole stalking bullshit in the first place. I'll do it. You can try me. I have a feeling I'd enjoy stalking the hell out of you." He smiled. It was naughty and full of promise.

She snatched her hand away. "There is nothing going on with me. I can't take this further… that's all!"

"Why not?"

With a noise of frustration, she turned, ran a few strides and shifted. She needed to get away. He needed to stop pursuing this. If she told him what was going on with her, he'd try to change her mind – might even get it right – that could only end in disaster. Plain and simple. Disaster.

Cordia took to the air, cursing inwardly when she heard clothing rip behind her. The dragon planned on following her. He was shifting too. *Why?* It was futile. She could fly circles around him for half the night and outrun him in an instant. She raced away. Not so fast that he wouldn't keep up, but fast enough that he would have to work hard to keep up… and work he did. His great wings flapped seemingly tirelessly. He'd said he would pursue this. Cordia got the feeling he meant it. It wasn't all just hot air. She made him chase her for a good long while just to be sure. It was just as she suspected. He didn't give up the chase. Didn't falter or slow. He kept on going. Kept on trying. He would follow her around the world. Would follow her home. Would stalk – what is it he had said? Stalk the hell out of her.

With a sigh, she slowed, looking for a place to land. They were in the middle of nowhere. Darkness all around. It was beautiful. Desolate and lonely too. It was perfect.

Maybe it would serve as a reminder of how her life had to remain… and maybe the opposite was true. Maybe the crushing beauty of the desolation and loneliness would push her into something new. Something that would spell disaster.

Death.

Maybe some things were worse. Cordia slowed her strokes, lowering herself, the long grass crushing under the pads of her paws as she landed. The great dragon landed beside her. Although he was no match for her, she was astounded by his size and strength. She screeched, giving one last-ditch effort to get him gone. Stone roared right back, making it clear he wasn't going to back down. These dragons were underestimated by her species. They could be a formidable foe.

His scales gleamed in the moonlight. Gorgeous amethyst eyes peered at her with intelligence and question. He hadn't expected her to give in.

Cordia was the first to shift. Stone was obviously afraid she would take off again if he did so first. Only once she was fully in her skin did he shift too. "I have to say," his voice was deep and gruff. His vocal cords still remembering his animal. They were still molded to make guttural sounds. "You look just as good in your animal form. Very impressive." His eyes held hers.

"The only reason I let you catch me." Her own voice was more high-pitched than normal. Still remembering her griffin. "The only reason I stopped was that I knew you meant it when you said you would keep pursuing this."

"Damn straight. You played that stalking card, so I'll use it."

"Stop with the whole stalking nonsense."

"You started it."

He was upset about it. Cordia could see that now. Even if he hadn't let on earlier, it was there. "You're right. I did and I'm sorry," she mumbled the apology, keeping her eyes on his.

"What's that, Feral? Dragons are hard of hearing."

She laughed, unable to hold back. Stone had that effect on her. "If you're hard of hearing. I'm slow and decrepit. You heard what I said. I'm sorry! There. I said it again. I shouldn't have said that you stalked me. It isn't true. I panicked. It was the first thing that came to mind."

Stone nodded. The male looked amazing surrounded by the dark, with a shower of stars to highlight his skin, his eyes, his hair. He took a step towards her and his muscles rippled and roped. "Why did you say it then?" There it was. The hurt. The uncertainty. It must be hard on a male like Stone who probably never felt uncertain of anything. He was brave, strong, a natural leader and very good-looking. There was a confidence about him. It bordered on arrogance, at times even overstepping the mark. This was different. This was shy and unsure. This was a side, she surmised, that he didn't know about himself. The vulnerable side. He was showing it to her. She felt warm inside. She felt herself soften but caught it and put a stop to it. He deserved something from her.

"I panicked because we can't be together. It can't happen. I needed you to stop trying to pursue this. I needed you to stop pursuing me. Not because of you, or anything you did or said, but because of me. I get the feeling you will try to fix it. I don't think it's something that can be fixed, or handled, or managed. You will want to do all of those things and it just isn't possible. I can't have you trying to talk me into... anything."

"Why are you pushing me away? What is it I'll try to fix? I can see nothing in need of fixing." He gave her the once-over. "You are amazing. Perfect just the way you are."

"You see!" She couldn't help smiling. "It's that... exactly that kind of talk that will get us into trouble."

"No more cryptic answers. I want the whole explanation. No holds barred."

"Okay." She nodded once, licking her lips. "Where do I start?"

"At the beginning, maybe."

"I lied to you. Well sort of. You assumed something and I didn't correct you. I allowed you to assume it. I let myself get carried away that first time. It's been a very long time since I was with a male. Then it happened again. The second time..." She shook her head. "It was wrong of me to let things get as far as they have, but you are right. Despite knowing very little about you. I felt it. A connection. A spark between us. A pull. It has only grown stronger."

"I knew it," he growled, grinning.

"It doesn't change anything, Stone. We can't try to see where this goes because it can't go anywhere. I lied to you when I said I was infertile." She blurted it out. It needed to be said. She was sure to keep her eyes on his. They widened for a few seconds.

Stone frowned. "What? You're not but..." He shook his head. "Why would you lie about a thing like that?"

She pushed out a breath. "I may not be infertile, but I may as well be." She shrugged. "So, it is partly true."

"That's insane thinking. Why? I don't understand." He

shook his head.

"Yesterday, each species presented on the fertility problems pertaining to their own kind."

"Yes, the fertile Feral females became sick when they were... pregnant and subsequently died. Your species — just like ours and all the others — is highly driven to procreate. All of your fertile females died from this sickness." She could see he was thinking it through. "There are only infertile females and elders left."

"Not true! There is one fertile female left."

"One." She could see him put it all together. His eyes widening and his mouth dropping open.

"No!" he breathed out the word.

"Yes." She nodded. "Namely, me. I have kept my distance from males all these years. I hardly ever give in to sex. I've gone there a handful of times over the last twelve years... slightly more than twelve but who's counting? I've done that to avoid this from happening."

"Feelings. A relationship. Love."

"Exactly." She sucked in a breath. "I should not be having sex at all... ever. I don't go into heat often and I can usually feel when it's about to happen but not always. It's risky." She was speaking quickly. "I'm also wired to procreate, as are you. We'll convince ourselves that it's okay and then I'll die a slow, painful death." Her breathing was ragged. Her eyes were wide. Her palms sweaty.

Holy fuck! No wonder she didn't want anything to do with what was happening between them. *No fucking wonder.* "You lost friends? Family?"

Her eyes welled with tears. "Yes." One ran down her

cheek. "I had to watch them all die. One after the other. My sister…"

"I remember, you told me about her." He assumed it was something else that had killed her, something more… normal. Now he could understand why Cordia was taking this so hard.

"Yes," she nodded. "We were close. That's why I could comprehend your pain. Your sister took her own life and yet… I can… I can understand why…" Her voice cracked and a flood of tears streamed down her cheeks.

"I'm so… I'm sorry…" He gripped her jaw with his hand, using his other hand to wipe away her tears. "Shit." He wrapped his arms around her, pulling her in close. "No wonder. I can't blame you for feeling the way you do. Why didn't you tell me?"

She shrugged, crying harder, her shoulders shaking. "I didn't want you to see me… to see me… as broken." She pulled back. Her eyes were red and tear-soaked. "I don't know why. I guess I wanted you that first time. If I told you, you would have run a mile. Most males do. Most males won't look my way at all. I'm ignored like I have a sickness because I do."

"No fucking way," he growled, feeling angry. "I don't believe it. A female like you." He looked her up and down.

"If I become with clutch I will die. Mounting can quite literally kill me. What kind of male wants a female like that?"

"I do!" He gripped her hips.

"No, you don't. I lied to you. I accused you of being a stalker. You should be running. Looking at me like I have a sickness. I am to be shunned and ignored." Another tear tracked down her cheek and his heart broke. It splintered into a hundred shards just hearing her words.

They cut at him. "No! That's not true. You have so much to offer. I don't see you in that way."

"You should, because it is true." She nodded.

"No, it doesn't have to be. I am not a Feral male. It could be different."

"Could be. Might be." She shook her head. "We have no way of knowing if that is true. The only way would be to go down a path that could lead to death and destruction. I have seen where that path leads. I'm not willing to go there. I can't!" She shook her head, fear etched in her eyes. "I have already put myself at risk. More so in the last two days than over the last decade. It has to stop!"

"We won't have young then. I wanted you even when I was sure you were infertile. You know that." Desperation ate at him.

She nodded once. "You're right in that, but how long would it last? What if a mistake was made? What if I became pregnant anyway? My best friend is trying for a child when she knows it might kill her." She shook her head. "We sometimes do stupid things in the name of love. We are sometimes driven to do stupid things."

"No! It doesn't have to be like that. I want you and you want me. Why can't we be together? Just *be*, dammit."

"I don't want to die, Stone. Being with you could spell death."

"It could spell so much more." He cupped her jaw again. "It could spell a future… and love. It could spell the end to loneliness for us both."

"You are not lonely. Don't even go there. You could go on one of those Hunts." She sounded anguished. Like the thought was abhorrent to her. "You could win one of the humans. A male like you could do it easily. You could have everything."

"I already do. She's standing right in front of me."

"We only met yesterday," she whispered.

"I don't care!" He clenched his teeth. "I don't care for the Hunt. I don't want to find a female that way. I'm lonely. I was lonely. I don't want to feel that way again and I don't think you do either. I would be able to scent if you were going into heat. We can use condoms and contraceptives."

"Human methods." She shook her head. Not convinced.

"I swear they work. I swear. Please can we try? Can we just discuss the possibilities? I'm falling for you, Cordia. Call it stalking." He felt his lips hint at a ghost of a smile. "Call it what you like. I don't care. I'm mad about you. I want to get to know you. Everything about you. I would hate anything to ever happen to you. I swear we can work around this. Do you trust me?"

It took longer than he would have liked, but he finally saw a flicker of something in her eyes. She nodded. "I do."

CHAPTER 14

Thank god!

A rush of air left him. "Thank you. I want you to come back home with me tomorrow. We can go and see one of the doctors living with us. A human doctor."

"Human?" She narrowed her eyes. "I'm still not convinced. What do humans know about species? Specifically, about the Feral?"

"Granted, not much. That's why I want you to come with me." He took both her hands. "She can check you over and give you an oral contraceptive."

"Oral…" Her eyes were lifted in thought. "Oh… yes… oral." She nodded.

"I'll organize a whole lot of condoms as well." He winked at her. "I want you to see our lair. To meet my friend Sand and his mate Macy… you'll like her. Am I going too fast for you?" He could see she looked a bit shell-shocked. "Tell me to slow down and I will… but I don't want to." He squeezed her hands.

"You *are* going fast. It makes me feel a touch dizzy." She swallowed thickly. "But I don't want you to slow down." She smiled. "I'm scared but I'm also very excited."

"Does that mean you'll leave with me? Spend a few days at the lair?" Hopefully, he could convince her to stay longer than that. Then they could visit her side of the world as well.

She nodded. "Yes, I will."

He put his arms around her and pulled her in close. "I'm so glad. I'm so happy you told me what was going on. It's completely understandable that you would feel the way you do."

"I knew you would talk me into pursuing this. You know it's still risky, right?"

He pulled back. "The risk can be minimized to a negligible level. I'm sure we might even be able to get it down to nothing." He raised his brows.

She nodded once. "Let's talk to your healers."

"We'll take things slow in the meanwhile."

She cocked her head and looked at him like he had turned green with pink polka dots.

"Okay, okay." He chuckled. "We can slow down. How's that?"

"Considering the speed at which we're going here, slowing down would be still be moving fast."

"Point taken. How about this? No sex until we know you're safe? You don't scent like you're about to go into heat or anything, but we won't take chances."

She nodded. "As much as I would love to keep having sex with you… I think it's a better idea." Cordia looked disappointed.

"I think it's a fantastic opportunity for plenty of

foreplay." He bobbed his brows.

"You and your foreplay." She shook her head, laughing.

"Fooling around can be fun too." He gripped her hips.

"I have no doubt." Her gaze dipped to his mouth and then back up.

Stone leaned in and kissed her, loving how she felt against his mouth. Loving the taste of her, the feel of her. Her hard nipples rubbed up against his chest. He could scent her arousal. Fucking delicious. He pulled back, his cock was hard, pressing against her belly.

"What did you have in mind?" Her eyes were bright and beautiful, just like the rest of her.

"I was thinking I'd like to suck on your clit. I'm good with my hands."

She threw her head back and laughed. "Your confidence is astounding. I will ease you with my mouth as well. I don't mind going first." She palmed his cock and Stone grunted loudly. *Shit!* Cordia was good with her hands too. He had a much better idea, though. "What is it?" She continued to palm his dick, her hand moving from base to tip. "You look like you had some sort of revelation."

He groaned as she cupped his balls, giving them a light squeeze. "I did! Shit, that feels good." He groaned again, gritting his teeth. "I know how we can both come at the same time without having sex. Although I'm not going to last if you keep that up."

Cordia let him go and Stone had to put a hand over his dick to stop himself from coming right then. Just the thought of what they were about to do, coupled with the way she had just rubbed his cock, made him hornier than a herd of cattle. He felt his chest rise and fall in quick succession. Need rushing through him. The scent of her arousal was now in full force. Both slightly salty and very sweet. Like salted caramel with a scoop of ice-cream. Stone was suddenly hungry as fuck.

"No sex, though." Her eyes were wide

"No sex." He shook his head. "Not until you're safe and ready." He let his eyes dip down, taking in her gorgeous body. "You're so damned sexy."

"What is your plan, then?"

"It's called a 69. Have you ever heard of a 69?"

She shook her head. "Never."

"I'll lie down on my back and you straddle me."

"That would be mounting." She frowned.

"No, not like that. Your pussy would be over my mouth, which would put your mouth—"

"Oh…" She breathed out the word. "I understand. I can't wait to get your prick in my mouth. Ferals don't have a gag reflex."

Jesus H!

He had died and gone to heaven. His balls clenched. This was going to be the quickest orgasm he had ever had. His balls were already in his throat.

"Lie down, dragon."

Stone did what she said and lay down on the grass. It was a bit prickly against his back, but he didn't care. "I'm not sure how you feel about… swallowing." This conversation had to happen. He respected Cordia and needed her to know that. "I will warn you before I come. I don't mind if you use your hand to finish me off."

"What would be the point of that? I will finish what I start." She smiled at him from under her lashes. "Lie

down, dragon. I am eager to be eased. I think you are too."
Her eyes moved down… down… down… landing on his
cock, which felt like it grew even harder.

Cordia went down on all fours and crawled on her
hands and knees towards him. He was about to become
the first dragon male to die from a heart attack. That, or
death by blood loss, since most of it was in his cock right
about then. "Cordia," he growled. It was another strangled
half-warning, half-plea.

The Feral smiled and continued to crawl down his body
before throwing her leg over his face, putting her hairless
pussy directly above him. Her sex glistened with her need.
It was flushed a dark pink and so inviting that he had to
lick his lips. He couldn't wait to climb right in. Couldn't
wait to hear all the noises she would make.

Stone sniffed loudly. "Salted caramel," he moaned,
before taking another nose-full.

"What," she giggled, "are you talking about? Are you
hungry?"

"Very fucking hungry. It's what you scent of… your
arousal."

"Salted caramel. Is that good to eat? It doesn't sound
good."

"Oh yes! It's good and I'm hungry as hell." He palmed
her ass, wanting her closer. He practically salivated,
desperate for a taste.

Cordia lowered herself, hovering just above his reach.
He could feel her hot breath fanning his dick. He squeezed
his eyes shut as the anticipation built. Then her mouth
closed over his head and he grunted. Loudly.

Cordia swirled her tongue over his head, and he
snarled. *For fuck sake!* It didn't get too much better than

this. This female may not have sex very much. She might not know much about foreplay either, but she was good.

She giggled and he felt her nipples bounce against him in time with her laugh. "Aren't you supposed to ease me at the same time? Isn't that how it works?"

Stone hadn't noticed that her pussy was practically plastered against his face. Feeling her mouth around his girth had been all-consuming. "Abso-fucking-lutely!" he growled, closing his mouth over her swollen clit.

Cordia sucked in a ragged breath and moaned.

He kept up the suction, using his tongue to move back and forth over her nub in slow, easy strokes. Her back bowed and she tried to move away but he held on tight.

"By the gods… so good," she moaned, her hips rocking.

Stone hooked his arm around her ass to keep her in place and sought out her slit with his now free hand. Her pussy was soaking wet. He had to squeeze his eyes shut as he imagined his dick taking the place of his fingers. Stone eased two inside her. They slipped in easily as she was good and wet.

Her pussy tugged him in deeper. Her velvet walls tight around him. He crooked his fingers just a little, so that they were brushing her upper wall. It wasn't hard to find the right spot because she soon cried out with a high-pitched melodic keen.

That's it!

Right there!

She wriggled and moaned and bucked against him. Then she sucked on his dick. This time, much harder and deeper than before. His balls moved straight to his throat and everything in him tightened. Cordia palmed the base of his cock and sucked on him again, making whimpering noises. He had to remind himself to keep finger-fucking her while keeping his hips still. It wasn't easy, considering how amazing her mouth felt, how decadent she tasted. Salted caramel was his new favorite.

He was shocked when her pussy tightened around his fingers and she groaned loudly. Her back bowed and she released his dick. Her pussy pulled even tighter and her groan became drawn out, sounding like it was coming from between her teeth. Her hips pumped against his hand. He kept up the suction on her clit, keeping her there.

Cordia groaned loudly, muttering his name and what sounded like curses. He laved her nub, suckling it again, softer this time while she came down.

"No more." She finally slumped against him. Cordia was panting hard. "So much for coming at the same time. I couldn't last. I love whatever it is you did with your fingers."

"Duly noted." He chuckled. "Wait until I ease the tip of my thumb into your ass at the same time."

"What?" Cordia sounded shocked. "You can't be serious." She also sounded very interested.

"I am. You're going to love it."

"Your turn." She picked herself up, leaning on her elbows and took his cock back into her mouth. One hand worked his base while the other played with his sack. She deep-throated him. As in fucking deep. No holds barred. No gag-fucking-reflex indeed. Her pussy was still in his face. Wet with her juices. He could glimpse down the narrow space between their bodies. Her nipples touched his stomach. Between her breasts, he could see her lips around him. Her hands on him. It was the most erotic thing he had ever seen before. Her mouth made suction noises as she moved up and down. He could feel the sweat roll down his face. As much as he wanted to come, he didn't want this to end. Torture and bliss, to the point of pain.

"I'm close," his words were almost unrecognizable. He hoped she would understand him. "I'm going to… come… soon."

Thank fuck, she didn't stop. Instead, she lowered the hand on his sack and massaged the sensitive patch of skin behind his balls. Cordia took him deeper. All the way to the back of her throat. His cock actually hit home. Stone all out snarled as his seed erupted. Again, he had to fight the urge to pump into her mouth. He worked hard at staying still. At letting her do the work. His eyes were wide. His mouth slack. He was grunting and groaning with each slurpy suction on his cock. Seconds later he touched the back of her head, threading his fingers through her hair. "Thank you," he growled. "That's officially the best head I've ever had." She released him with a soft pop.

Her hair was mussed. Her cheeks a rosy color. Her eyes seemed to glow.

She crawled over to him and curled up against him. Stone pulled her in close. "See, I'm sure this can work. That was… amazing. You're some female."

When she didn't say anything, he glanced down at her. Cordia was looking up at the stars. A sad expression on her face. Like she didn't believe they could get through this. She certainly mistrusted humans and what they were capable of. He was sure Meghan would change her mind. Sand's sister-in-law was an amazing doctor. If anyone could help them, it was her. He considered talking to

Druze as well, but it might bring up painful memories for the male.

"What was your sister like?" Cordia asked.

He looked up as well at the twinkling blanket above them. "Amethyst was beautiful. Inside and out. She was timid and very sweet. She was kind and always put others first. What about your sister?"

"Lorlian was the complete opposite." Cordia laughed, her eyes dancing. "She was feisty. You think I'm bad, well, she was ten times worse. It is not known but a handful of females survived the sickness."

"Really?' He lifted their brows. "I thought they all died." His heart leaped. Maybe they *did* have a chance.

"They had the eggs cut out from them with a silver blade. Of course, the eggs did not survive. The females who went that route are infertile today after having their reproductive organs ravaged by silver. They didn't technically survive the illness. There is no cure. Many females who went that route did not survive. Most died from blood loss. At least their death was swifter." Cordia seemed to compose herself, swallowing hard. "Lorlian wouldn't hear of it. She refused to sacrifice her young. She said she would fight until her last breath and that's what she did. She was so strong and courageous and brave."

"Surely if there was a chance at survival, you would take it?" He was thinking of Cordia and not her sister.

"One in ten lived. That's not great odds."

"It's something."

"And sometimes a female's motherly instincts are too strong." Cordia shrugged. "I understand why Lorlian made the choices she made. I would do the same."

He rubbed her back, wanting to pull her in closer.

They'd had unprotected sex. Stone was sure Cordia hadn't been in heat but what if—*Fuck!* He couldn't think along those lines. "What do you say we head back? I would love to curl up in bed with you. To hold you close all night long." He tucked some hair behind her ear.

"We're supposed to be taking it slow." She smiled. "I would love that, though."

"You would? You're sure? I can back off. I would hate for you to get me into even bigger shit for stalking you."

She laughed. "You're never going to let me live that down."

"Nope." He shook his head. "I'm afraid not. I want to talk some more. I want to know more about you."

"I'm not a good talker. I've kept to myself over the years. I don't speak to males at all."

He chuckled. "I know this is going to make me sound like a dick, but I'm glad. I get jealous at the idea of any other male near you. Also, it explains your reaction to me when I first entered the conference room. I honestly thought I'd done something terrible, like kick a puppy on the way in without knowing it."

"I was attracted to you immediately and it irritated me."

Stone chuckled. "I was attracted to you too. Your anger and bristliness attracted me just as much as your beauty. I couldn't help but wonder who the sexy creature was across from me, the one with murder in her eyes. I was a little scared and a lot turned on. Sick, I know."

"Scared for good reason. I think this was the first time I didn't break you."

He laughed. "I love being broken by you, Cordia. I'm aiming for every bone in my body. At least then I'll know I'm doing a good job."

"You're crazy." She laughed as well. "It has to hurt."

"Crazy for you and I don't care about the pain." He winked.

"Crazy and cheesy." She laughed harder.

He loved hearing it. Loved seeing her so carefree. It was the first time she'd let her guard down. They were going to be okay. He just knew it.

CHAPTER 15

C ordia's eyes were huge. "Wow! It's beautiful. One big nest," she whispered. Not a nest. The dragons called it a lair. There were many nests built into the side of a cliff. Large balconies jutted from each nest. They had landed on one a few moments earlier.

"I take it things are different where you come from?" Stone asked, after shifting back into his human form. His eyes were on her.

She nodded. "Yes. We have many nests. Some Feral choose to live close to others, while others prefer seclusion. But each nest stands on its own. This is strange to me, but I like it. It's still open and off the ground. You can shift and leave whenever you want." She ran her eyes over the many balconies and windows.

"Good to hear. I will enjoy visiting Feral lands and seeing how things are for myself."

"I will enjoy taking you."

"Let's go inside." Stone gestured to a large door. "This is my chamber… or nest, as you would call it."

"Why are those balconies so much bigger?" She pointed at the largest one. It seemed many dragons came and went using that balcony.

"That leads to the public areas. Like the great hall and the library."

"Oh… I would love to see them as well." She watched as a dragon landed on the large space.

He nodded. "You will. I will take you all around." Stone took her hand. "But first… let's go inside and get dressed." He gave her a small pull.

"I don't like wearing clothing. Do we have to put them on? I had hoped once the conference was over to be able to relax."

"Dragons cover up. We only strip to shift." His eyes darkened.

"What if I wore a skirt. Ferals go naked or cover the bottom half only."

"I don't like the idea of the males in my tribe looking at you naked or even topless." His voice sounded gruff. His jaw clenched.

"Why not? I am not so different from a male. I am tall. I am muscled… not nearly as muscled as you but—"

"You have a vagina and breasts." He sounded… angry. "You are very different to a male."

"They are small." She cupped her mammary glands.

"They are bigger than any male I know and your nipples are plump. Very different to how a male looks."

"Oh." It made her feel warm inside. "I was worried I wasn't soft and feminine enough for you," she teased. It was something she had thought about a couple of times.

"You are a female through and through. I like how toned and strong you are. You have a tight ass and the longest legs I have ever seen. Your breasts fit my mouth perfectly." He gave her a half-smile which quickly turned serious. "The males in my tribe would be all over you if you walked out of here naked. I would end up fighting. Possibly even gouging out eyes."

"Jealous?" She smiled.

"Yes!" he growled, "I am."

She nodded. "Good, I am glad to hear it. I was very jealous when I saw you with Helga and Lexi. I wanted to tear Helga's arm off when she touched you."

"So," he folded his arms, "you finally admit to being jealous."

She nodded. "I do. Let's go and get dressed then."

He nodded. "We have a meeting with a healer in half an hour."

Her eyes widened. "Wow! That's quick."

"I spoke to Doctor Meghan on the phone earlier today and she said that the medication to stop pregnancy can take a couple of weeks to work properly. I wanted to get the ball rolling. I know we have agreed to take it slow, but I am desperate to be inside you again." He hooked an arm around her waist. "I love your mouth and your hands but I want you, all of you. Don't be afraid, please, but I want to mate you. I know already that you are the right female for me. It feels like you were meant to be mine."

She bit her lip. *Tar and feathers.* Even though her heart beat faster, she didn't feel afraid. She should, but she didn't. "I know what you mean. This feels right. Us."

He nodded. "Exactly. When we mate, Cordia… it has to be skin to skin, so those pills need to be working. After that, we can go back to using condoms all of the time."

"Well," she smiled. "We'd better get ready for the healer then. So much for taking it slow." She laughed.

He nodded and then chuckled. "Shew! I was sure you were going to run. It is going to take time for those pills to work. We won't be able to go without condoms any time soon. Let's hear what the healer has to say and we'll take it from there. One step at a time."

She nodded. "One step at a time."

Meghan positioned the sonar wand on Cordia's belly. The doctor looked at the screen, making noises that sounded like she was interested in what she was seeing. Then repositioned the device, making more of such noises. Cordia's belly was covered in a sticky gel which apparently helped Meghan see into her. It didn't hurt at all.

The doctor put the handheld-device down, she removed her gloves, moving over to her computer where she typed something in.

"Is everything okay?" Cordia asked. She positioned herself onto her elbows. This didn't look good.

"Yes, all fine." Meghan looked up smiling. "I'm just not exactly sure of what I'm seeing… although I can guess." She took in a deep breath, glancing down at the screen for a second. "Your reproductive system is a mixture between human and avian. It leans more towards avian. So, a combination of oviparous and viviparous."

"I'm sorry." Cordia shook her head. "What is avian? And ovi…" She let the sentence die, widening her eyes and making a face.

"Yeah, doc," Stone said. "English please."

"I'm sorry." Meghan laughed. "Your system is a mix between a bird's and a human."

"We produce eggs in a clutch of three," Cordia explained.

"Will that affect birth control?" Stone asked, frowning.

The healer raised her brows, looking unsure.

"Like I said," Meghan addressed Cordia. "You are a mix of both *human* and bird. I may need to do some research and to consult with an avian veterinarian. In the meanwhile..." She stood up from her desk and headed to a door on the other side of the room. She opened it, staring into a well-stocked cupboard housing medical supplies. "Here we go." She pulled out a large box, handing it to Stone. "I take it you know how to use condoms." She'd passed him a box of the rubber coverings.

He nodded once, glancing at Cordia. "I do."

"Will they work, Meghan... um... doctor?" Cordia asked, still feeling unsure about this. She wasn't a human.

Stone clasped her hand giving it a squeeze. "We would rather wait if there is any chance of anything going wrong."

"This clutch sickness you described is very serious. I will discuss what I can with the avian vet without giving too much away. Maybe he or she can shed some light on what could have caused this. Your species never consulted with humans, did you?"

Cordia shook her head. "We did not believe that humans could help us. You did not... most humans still do not even know of our existence. Perhaps that was flawed thinking."

"Hindsight is foresight." Meghan's eyes softened. "It's easy to look back and then decide that things could have been done differently. You have to do the best that you can in the moment and then learn from it."

"I learned I can never become with clutch." Cordia shook her head. The idea terrified her. Clutch sickness was a terrible thing. "I can never have young but maybe I don't have to be alone like I initially predicted." She looked up at Stone and smiled, feeling warm inside.

Stone squeezed her hand again, smiling back.

"You don't have to be alone," Meghan said. "But you do both need to be extra careful. You can't have sex without using a condom. I know dragons have a fantastic sense of smell but…" She shook her head. "Things sometimes go wrong. I do believe that your sense of smell," she looked at Stone, "combined with using these," she tapped on the box in Stone's hand, "will be sufficient until we have a contraceptive for you. Once that happens, I doubt very much that you would become pregnant… with clutch, unless it was something you actually tried for."

"You're sure?" Cordia narrowed her eyes. It couldn't be this simple. Something had to give.

"As long as a condom didn't break, which, can happen. It's a risk you would need to take."

"How long before you could have a contraceptive for Cordia?"

"That's hard to say." She shook her head. "It could be a week or two. It could also be months."

Cordia squeezed her eyes shut. Months. She prayed it wasn't the case.

"Okay, thank you, doctor. I appreciate it."

"Yes," Cordia nodded. "Thank you."

"I'll get back to you as soon as I have any news."

They left, walking in silence for a time. The hallways were especially busy. Everybody stopped to stare as they walked by. There were far more males than females, Cordia noted. A similar situation to that of the Feral. Thankfully, Stone had an arm around her. He pulled her in closer every time someone leered.

They finally made it back to his chamber. Stone closed the door behind them.

"That was a little odd," Cordia remarked.

"Yeah, it sure was." He put his arms around her. "I think my species are curious about you. I had never seen a Feral before meeting you. I am sure that is true of most of my people. I hope it doesn't weird you out?"

She shook her head. "It is understandable."

"I'm sure they'll get used to you very quickly. It was the same when we brought human females into our lair for the first time. All the males were scrambling to catch a glimpse."

"I'm sure." She pushed out a breath, pulling away to go and sit on the edge of the sofa. Cordia wrapped her arms around herself. She had hoped for better news. She'd also felt that they should be taking it slower. This was forcing just that. Their relationship was so new. Only a few days. Yet, it felt like she'd known Stone forever.

"How do you feel about our meeting with Meghan?" Stone went and sat next to her, he took her hand, waiting patiently for her to reply.

"I'm not sure." She pushed out a solid breath. "I was hoping things would be a little more cut and dry but, I guess, it is what I expected. We are different to humans. We're very different. Vampires, elves and even shifters are similar, but we Feral…" She shook her head slowly. "We're part avian." She smiled. "I learned a new word today."

Stone nodded and smiled back, it was tight. "I didn't expect that. I really believed you'd be given the pills and we'd be on our way. I can understand why Meghan is being so cautious. I'm glad, since your life is very much at stake."

"Clutch sickness is awful. I know I keep harping on about it, but I can't help it. It doesn't matter how many years have passed, I can still remember those dark days. Friends, family, my sister…" She shook her head. Cordia's eyes stung. Her throat felt clogged. She pulled in a deep breath, trying to find calm.

"We'll wait," Stone said, sounding resolute. "I don't care if it takes months… years… Your pussy tastes that damned good." He leaned in and kissed the side of her mouth. He was trying to be flippant, but she could hear the edge to his voice. His eyes were filled with concern as they held hers.

His phone started ringing but he silenced it without checking who was calling.

Cordia smiled. "As much as I like that thing you did with your fingers and that other thing you did with your thumb in the shower this morning," she felt her cheeks heat at how hard she had come, "I think we should try the rubber coverings." She nodded too quickly. Cordia forced herself to stay still instead.

He frowned. "Are you sure? I don't know. I think we—"

"The doctor seemed to think it would be okay. You said it would be fine when we discussed it last night. You will most likely scent if I go into heat, won't you?"

He nodded too quickly, looking nervous… make that terrified. His eyes had a glassy look. His jaw was tight.

"You said that the coverings work well? They will trap your seed?"

"Yeah, but they do sometimes break or tear." He widened his eyes. "It can happen. You know that, right?"

"Not very often, though?" she countered. They needed to try. The healer seemed okay with it. If they were going to make a go of this, she needed to be brave and they needed to explore new possibilities together. That's what being partners was about. She knew this was risky going into it, but Stone was worth it.

"No, but they weren't designed to have that whole suction thing happen."

"It isn't too hard is it?" She frowned. Some of the things Helga and Lexi had said came back to her. She knew she shouldn't listen to the two of them, but it was tough sometimes. "Did I hurt you?" There, it was out.

He shook his head and groaned. She felt the sound he made deep inside her. Her nipples hardened up as well. "No, not at all. The opposite is true. I love it! Addictive comes to mind." He winked at her.

Good! Her heart resumed beating. She had been sure he would say something like that, yet there had been a part of her that had been worried. "I'm sure it would be okay if we had sex then." She chewed on her lip. "Maybe we can take it slow and easy. Do plenty of that foreplay first." She licked her lips.

His phone started ringing again. Stone glanced down, frowning. He switched it off this time.

"That might be important." She pointed at the device.

"Nothing is more important than this right now."

Her heart began to beat against her chest. Her whole body warmed. She wanted to feel close to Stone. "You could get me really wet." Cordia parted her legs just a little, shimmying her skirt up and up, until her sex was only just hidden. He might take some convincing. He still looked unsure and worried, which made her even more sure.

His nostrils flared. She knew he would be able to scent her arousal. Just thinking of them mounting had her feeling achy and needy.

Stone looked like he was about to say something. He even began shaking his head, but his eyes were between her legs, even though he wouldn't be able to see anything. Cordia gave a little circling thrust of her hips. "You could mount me slow and easy. Take your time. Make me beg." She licked her lips again, still doing the thrusting, circling movement she could see he liked.

"Now look what you've done," Stone groaned, looking down. His prick was rock hard. It tented his pants. "Are you sure?" He was frowning hard. His face was pinched. His mouth tight. "We can wait. I swear I don't mind." He grit his teeth, looking her in the eyes.

"Do I scent any different to you?"

He shook his head.

Cordia pulled her skirt up around her hips as she straddled him. "Get one of those condom coverings." She looked at the box on the table next to them.

Stone raised his brows. "What about foreplay?" He rubbed on her swollen nub, dipping his finger into her channel, using the juices to lubricate his finger before moving back to her clit. He slipped and slid all over the small bundle of nerves. Cordia's eyes drifted shut and she moaned. He knew exactly how to touch her. Exactly how hard or soft. How fast or slow. He knew what she needed at that moment and gave it to her.

Her snatch clenched, she could feel herself growing wetter. He pushed two fingers inside her. She groaned, unable to stop the building need that clawed at her. Stone growled low. A vibrating rumble of arousal. He removed his fingers, only to start back on her tight nub. So soft, she rolled her pelvis to try to grind up against him. Needing more. Instead of fingers, her clit met with hard cock. Cordia ground herself against him. Ground herself against his cotton-clad steel.

"That's it." Stone's voice was tight. She opened her eyes staring into his glowing amethyst gaze. His lids were at half-mast. Already, she burned with the need to come, she rubbed herself harder against Stone's prick. He groaned.

"Shall I put the covering on?"

He grinned. It was tight with need. "I'll do it." He kept his finger on her clit. Just one teasing tip. Slowly circling the little nub. Round and round, driving her crazy. With one hand, he opened the box and pulled out a string of silver. Using his teeth, he tore off the end, pulling out – what looked like – a glob. How was this going to work? It could never fit over his prick. Surely?

The finger on her clit moved directly over the nerve bundle and began strumming. She groaned hard. Her eyes threatened to roll back and her back did bow some. She looked between them as he palmed his cock. At least, it looked like he was palming his cock, although he was actually covering it with the rubber. It was strange to see his member encased in the tight substance. "Does it hurt?" Her words were high-pitched with need. His finger had gone back to lazy circling, keeping her there but not taking her further.

He shook his head. "Not at all."

"Will it feel the same?"

"Not exactly the same, but close enough. You ready to give this a go?"

She swallowed thickly from both need and fear. "It looks too thin to hold."

"It's stronger than it looks." He kissed her slow and easy, his finger staying soft but insistent on her clit. Cordia groaned as they came apart.

She nodded, positioning him at her entrance, slipping in easily. Cordia eased down on his hard length, panting as he slowly filled her. Loving how she stretched to accommodate him.

Stone pushed up from below. She cried out with the pure ecstasy as he fully sheathed himself in her. She swallowed hard, rocking her hips, keeping him deep. Loving how he felt inside her. So connected in this moment.

Cordia eased up and pushed back down. They had to try to take this slow and careful. Stone groaned.

"That's it. You feel so good." His deep voice rolled over her.

Up and down, she leaned forward ever so slightly until she found that angle that hit her just right. She whimpered as she slid back down on him.

"Try a little faster," Stone urged her, keeping his hands on her hips. "You feel amazing."

Cordia opened her eyes, looking at Stone. His lashes were at half-mast, his mouth open. She did as he asked upping the tempo while still ensuring that she kept him deep. She mewled each time she slid back onto him. Stone thrust from below, keeping the rhythm she had set. Not too hard. Not too much.

"So good." His eyes were glowing lightly. So beautiful.

"I wish you could flip me over and mount me hard," she managed to push out.

Stone choked out a laugh, his breathing ragged. "We'll put it on our list of 'to do's,' for sure."

"I want to see you." He lifted her shirt and Cordia tugged it over her head. "Stunning," he growled. Up… down… up… down. Harder and faster with every bounce. Her mammary glands jiggled with each downward thrust. Maybe she wasn't as masculine as she had imagined. His eyes were glued to her chest. Stone seemed to enjoy what he saw.

Cordia concentrated on her own pleasure, knowing it would draw an orgasm out of him when they coupled inside her. She needed to come more than her next breath. The incredible slip and slide of his cock taking her closer and closer with every sweet thrust.

"That's it, my gorgeous Feral. Just a little more." He grit his teeth.

She cried out as his finger brushed against her clit. Stone's face was taut with desire.

"Oh yes," she cried. Her orgasm building as his finger picked up momentum over her tightening nub. When Stone pinched her clit between two fingers while thrusting slightly harder from below, it was as if she had died and gone to heaven. It was more than enough to have her screaming as waves of pleasure rushed through her. She barely registered Stone jerking beneath her as he found his own release. She felt herself close around the head of his prick, holding on almost too tightly. Stone roared. It sounded like she was hurting him. Killing him even. She was sure to keep her legs from closing and her hands from grabbing. The roar went on for a good few seconds. Long and drawn-out. Like he was dying or something. She knew better after their talk. It was a roar of pleasure. Sheer pleasure. This time she was sure.

Cordia felt her mouth tilt up in a smile as she slowed her movements. Stone's eyes were closed, and he lay back on the sofa. "You amaze me." His voice was husky and well-used.

She could feel herself easing as their coupling released deep inside her. This was it. Had the thin rubber stayed intact? It didn't seem possible. She slid off him. They both looked between them as his prick pulled free.

Cordia sighed in relief when she saw that it was undamaged, the end filled with seed. The thin material had done its job.

"What did I tell you?" Stone grinned. He leaned forward brushing his lips over hers. We just have to go nice and slow, with plenty of foreplay. He winked at her.

Cordia giggled. Maybe things would work out between them after all. "I think so." She nodded. "It sounds good." She ran a hand down his chest, tracing the silver marking.

"But first, my beautiful female, I must feed you. How does an early dinner sound, followed by some lovemaking?"

"Lovemaking?" She frowned. "How do you make some... love? Surely you feel it?"

Stone chuckled. "Making love is slow rutting with lots of foreplay. It is a way to show your partner what they mean to you." He was looking deep into her eyes, an intense expression on his face.

Her heart beat faster. Was he going to tell her that he loved her? By claw, from the way he was looking at her, it might just happen. She held her breath in anticipation. It was too soon but she wanted to hear it all the same. Cordia felt love for Stone. She felt it through and through. She was risking everything for him and doing so wholeheartedly. It might be reckless, but it was right.

"I plan on making plenty of love to you, Cordia," he finally said, kissing her again. Slowly and sweetly, taking her breath all over again. "First some food."

Stone lifted her off his lap and onto the sofa. Then he stood up himself. "Just have to take care of this first." He removed the condom, pulled his pants up, then headed for the bathroom. It took a minute or two for him to return. "What do you feel like eating?"

"Anything."

"I can make a mean elk pot pie." He winked at her.

She frowned. "How can a pot pie be mean? Surely the elk will be dead."

Stone choked out a laugh. "How did I get so lucky?" He picked up his phone, turning it on. "When I say mean, what I—" His phone beeped several times in quick session, interrupting what he was saying.

"Looks like someone has been trying to reach you," she remarked.

CHAPTER 16

The next evening...

"Oh my gosh," Macy giggled. "I can't believe it. You actually brought someone around. I'm Macy." She held out her hand to Cordia.

Cordia looked down at the outstretched hand and then up at Macy and then back down at the hand.

"Um," Stone touched the small of Cordia's back, "you're supposed to take someone's hand when they offer it to you and shake..."

"Oh!" Cordia widened her eyes. "Of course. I know that. I know. My best friend is a human. Vicky is..." She chewed on her lip, looking nervous and sounding nervous. He could see it. If she had a scent, he'd smell it on her too. Her skin was pale. She was worried about making a good impression. His female stopped babbling and took Macy's hand. The other female winced.

"Not too hard," Stone warned.

"Oh… of course," Cordia's voice was high-pitched. "I'm sorry, human… Macy. I'm sorry." Her shoulders slumped. "The truth is that I am anxious about meeting you, the two of you." She glanced at Sand and then back at Macy. "I know that you are good friends of Stone's, and I wanted to make a good first impression." Trust Cordia to be so direct.

He put his arm around her and pulled her in. "You *are* making a good first impression. Just like when we first met." He winked at her.

She turned, narrowing her eyes at him and he laughed.

Macy giggled and Sand smiled broadly. "Don't worry about all that. You must be an amazing woman. Stone has never so much as looked at a female in the time I have known him, let alone brought one around. That must make you special."

"We've only been together for six months, hun."

Macy elbowed Sand in the ribs. Sand choked out a laugh. "I'm kidding. Stone has never brought a female around. I've known him for many years. It is good to meet you." He shook her hand as well.

He could see Cordia relax, the worry lines around her mouth were gone and her eyes brightened up.

"So we finally get to celebrate," Stone announced. "We're pregnant." He looked down at Macy's belly and then back up at her face.

Macy smiled so broadly that he was sure he could see every tooth in her mouth. "We are!" she yelled.

"My female is going to have my young." Sand sounded like he was in awe. The male picked Macy up and twirled her around like he had just heard the news for the first time.

Macy giggled. "Put me down. We have guests. Sand, put me down right now before you make me queasy."

That did it. He put her down immediately, looking concerned. "Can I get you some of that ginger soda you like? Some crackers?"

Macy laughed. "I'm okay for now. No more spinning me around, though. I think maybe our guests would like something to drink."

"Are your males as protective when a female is pregnant?"

Cordia inhaled sharply, her eyes widening again.

"I'll have a beer," Stone interjected, hoping to stop the conversation in its tracks. "What about you?" He squeezed Cordia's hip.

"I... um... I..."

"What about a glass of wine?" Macy asked. "I'm not drinking," she rubbed her still flat belly, smiling, "for obvious reasons, but there is no reason why you can't have a glass."

"I have never had wine before." Cordia shook her head.

"I'll get Sand to pour you a glass and you can try. How's that?" Macy asked.

Cordia nodded.

"You were about to tell me if Feral males are as protective as dragon shifter males."

"They are." Cordia nodded. "Very much so."

Stone thanked Sand for the beer. He considered putting a stop to the conversation but decided to let it go. Cordia was more than capable of handling herself.

"How do Feral pregnancies work? Stone was telling me

that you are a griffin shifter," she lifted her eyes in thought, "which is half eagle and half lion, right? I mean, wow, how interesting! Do you have live young, or eggs?" Macy went on. They both thanked Sand when he delivered their drinks.

"Eggs," Cordia replied. "A clutch of three."

"Wow! Three? That's hectic. I thought two was rough." She rubbed a hand over her belly again. "Not that I'm complaining. We tried hard for these babies – technically from even before we were together, but that's a story for another day. I'm thrilled to finally be pregnant."

Sand tried to say something, but Stone waved him off, ready to jump in if Cordia needed him.

"So, the two of you might end up with three running around if you decide to have kids?" Macy raised her brows.

Shit! What should he do?

"No." Cordia shook her head. She looked calm. "I cannot have young."

"Oh." Macy shook her head, looking upset. "I'm so sorry." She looked up at Stone. "I didn't know. Here I am yammering on and on. You should have said something."

"I don't mind." Cordia took a sip of the wine and grimaced. "You are with child and very excited. I am happy to talk about pregnancy and babies with you. Not that I know very much. You can tell me all about it." She put the glass down.

Why had he even worried? Cordia handled that beautifully.

"We're going to have our hands very full in a couple of months." Macy looked over at Sand and the two of them shared a moment. Stone locked eyes with Cordia and winked. She smiled back.

"Hey, the two of you will have to babysit for us," Macy said, taking a sip of her juice. "You *do* know that, don't you?"

Cordia suddenly looked very afraid. "I wouldn't know the first thing about babies. I've never been around one. I—"

"That would be great," Stone said. "It isn't all that difficult." He kept his eyes on his female. "We can figure it out together. I'm sure the two of you will be able to give us plenty of tips." He laughed. "Come to think of it, you'll leave us a list of instructions about a mile long, Mace. Written down in bullet points."

"How can you write with the point of a bullet?" Cordia asked.

Sand chuckled and Macy did her best to hold back a laugh, as did he. Stone cleared his throat. "Bullet points means a list with dots at the start of each new item. I'll show you when we get home." *Shit!* He'd called his chamber home, as in hers as well.

Cordia just nodded.

Macy smiled. "I probably would leave you a whole list of instructions, and I might have a hard time leaving too."

"Don't worry, babe, I'd drag you out. We're going to need the odd date night. I've seen how it is with my brothers," Sand groaned. "I can't wait to be a dad, but I know I'll want some alone time with you."

"You're already planning alone time with me and they aren't even born yet."

Sand kissed the top of Macy's head. "What do you say we get the steaks and ribs on the barbeque?" He looked Stone's way.

"Sounds good." He followed Sand into the kitchen.

The male opened the fridge and took out the meat. He motioned to an empty tray. "You take that."

"Just a sec." Stone poured a glass of juice and retrieved the tray. He followed Sand, handing the glass to his female on the way out.

She gave him a look of gratitude.

"Not loving the wine?" Macy giggled. "Don't worry about it, it's an acquired taste."

By the time he got outside onto the balcony, Sand was already putting the ribs on the grill.

"So, why did it take you ten messages to answer my call?"

"Why did you call ten times?" Stone shook his head. "Who calls a person ten times?"

Sand chuckled. "Do you blame me?" He frowned. "Maybe I should ask you why you didn't tell me about… your female? You bring a female home. A Feral," he whispered the last, "and you don't tell me. Quite frankly, I was hurt. Still am." He clutched his chest dramatically.

"You're full of shit!" Stone laughed. "It all happened so quickly." He could feel he was smiling, knew that it was goofy, but he didn't give a shit.

"I'll say. You've known Cordia for a couple of days."

"Yep." Stone nodded.

"And you're fucking enamored. Like a puppy dog." Sand put the ribs on the grill.

"You're one to talk."

Sand nodded. "Yeah, that's true. I can't believe it, though. I was a little worried there myself for a while. I was starting to think it was never going to happen for you. Even our dragon females have shown tons of interest and you don't bite. The odd human on a stag run and that was it."

Stone gave him the stink eye. "It just had to be the right female for me to want to settle down."

"So, this is it?" The steak went on next.

"Yep, this is it. I know she's a little different." He shrugged. "She gets regular everyday sayings all wrong. She's cracked a few of my ribs." He winced. "And possibly my hip as well."

Sand choked out a laugh. "What?"

"I'm that good in the sack." He smirked and gave a one-shouldered shrug.

Sand rolled his eyes. "You are so damned full of it. And what about her being infertile? Doesn't that bother you?"

"No!" He shook his head. "And she's technically not infertile."

"What? I thought all the remaining Feral females were infertile. By the way," he spoke as he flipped the ribs over, "I should have told Mace. I forgot."

"Nah, it's fine. Let them sort themselves out."

"Okay, back to Cordia." He frowned. "You said she *can* have young. Why did she say that she can't?"

Stone explained the situation to Sand.

"That's rough." He shook his head. "Really rough. The Feral have been through so much." He looked at Stone pointedly and pushed a breath out through his nose. "You never know, there might be hope for the two of you. It can happen."

"Nah!" He shook his head. "I would never risk my female like that."

"The humans are really up to date with the latest technology. I'm telling you, it could be possible. Let

Meghan run tests. Maybe she can consult with experts. You never know, you should keep your mind open to the possibility, at least."

Stone took a sip of his beer, his mind working.

CHAPTER 17

The next morning…

"Go down onto your elbows and brace yourself." Stone gripped her hips as he spoke.

She whimpered as his tip breached her opening. Just the very tip.

Cordia did as he asked and lowered herself, braced against the mattress. Her face ploughed into the soft duvet as he thrust into her, right to the hilt. It took her breath away. Full and stretched to capacity in an instant. Good thing she was so wet from the foreplay. He had made her come with his mouth.

Stone didn't give her a chance to catch her breath, he kept driving into her using hard, powerful thrusts. The coiling sensation increased. She made moaning noises with each hard shove. The moans sounded choked. Her breasts were mashed up against the bedding. Her knees barely touching. Her snatch made a greedy suckling sound around his shaft.

Her eyes were wide. Her breath coming in pants. Her body was already tensing. More coiling. More heaviness. A louder, higher-pitched moan was torn from her. The sounds of his body slapping against hers filled the room. Her body made a wet suction noise each time he withdrew. This was sex in its most raw and primal form. It was better than all the sex she'd had to date all rolled into one.

Stone was grunting and groaning loudly. His hard breaths were almost as loud as her own. His fingers dug into her. He gripped a handful of her hair and pulled lightly as his body began to jerk into her. His movements turned frantic, his moans animalistic.

It was enough to send her spiraling out of control as well. She yelled into the bedcover as her body let go, clamping down on him. All that pent-up ecstasy coursed through her in a rush of pleasure so blinding it made her eyes water. Stone gave his signature roar and she felt bad for any nests in close proximity to theirs.

He jerked a few times before slowing. Then he caged her with his body, his head against her back. He was breathing heavily; they both were. "By claw and by scale, female," he mumbled against her skin.

It took a few more seconds for her to release him, but Stone stayed joined with her. When he finally withdrew it was with a loud curse.

"What is it?" Her voice was little croaky and a lot sleepy.

"It broke." He was holding his prick, which was a dripping mess where the rubber had split open. "I don't think very much went inside you and you don't scent any different."

Her heart raced and she couldn't take her eyes off the seed on the end of his prick. She forced herself to breathe and to calm down. It wasn't a big deal, and yet it was. Every time this happened it put her at further risk.

"I'm so sorry." Stone looked distraught. He ran a hand through his hair. His other hand still wrapped around his cock. "It's my fault. I got caught up. I was too rough, especially at the end."

She took a deep breath. "It's not your fault. It's the coupling at the end. I was worried it might—"

"Yeah." He pushed out the word. "I will need to be more careful. That's all."

"I don't know." She shook her head. "I think it's a bad idea."

"Okay." He nodded. "Like I said," he smiled, "I love tasting you."

"It could take months before the healers find a contraceptive medication that will work." She frowned. "We can't just stop having sex for all that time."

"I don't care how long it takes." He glanced down between his legs, a pained expression on his face. "Let me go and take care of this, I'll be back in a second." Stone got off the bed and headed for the adjoining bathroom. It didn't take long, and he reemerged. "I'm so damned sorry about what happened. I really should have been more careful." He climbed back onto the bed.

"Stop apologizing. It's not your fault. Good sex means getting caught up in the moment. I did too. Your sheets and blankets are all ripped to shreds. You didn't hear me complain. Sex is a big risk for me. It is why I fought so hard to prevent us from… from becoming attached. I am still worried that your healers won't find a solution for me… for us. I am not a human. The Feral are different from all the other species."

"We'll wait until they find one." He shrugged. "No big deal. I am a patient male. In the meanwhile, we get to spend plenty of time together." He winked at her, clutching onto her ankle in a soft hold. "We don't have to have sex. You never know, we can remain hopeful that a cure is found for your affliction. It could be possible, Cordia." He narrowed his eyes into hers. "Maybe one day we will even be able to have young. We need to keep positive and open-minded."

Dread filled her. *What was Stone saying?* "We spoke about this a few days ago. You told me you were comfortable with never having young. With never trying or even contemplating the notion."

"I am! Very comfortable… but why close ourselves off to the possibility? I would never risk you, Cordia." He shook his head. "Don't misunderstand me. After chatting to Sand last night and seeing Meghan, I was just reminded that there is advanced technology out there. That's all. I'm not pushing you into anything. I would never do that. Let's stay open-minded, that's all."

"I told you that it could never happen. I warned you." Her voice turned a little high-pitched, but she couldn't help it. Panic welled. "We aren't even mated yet and already you are talking about the possibility of young. There is no possibility. It will never happen." She shook her head and her chest heaved. "You need to accept that, and until your healer comes up with a medication that will work without fail, we cannot have sex again." She felt her eyes sting. "What kind of relationship is that?" She sniffed, working hard to hold back the emotions going wild inside her. "It is why I fought this in the first place. It is why I..." She shook her head. This wasn't going to work. She had been wrong to think any differently. To ever give herself hope.

"We will make do."

"Make do." It wasn't right. It wasn't normal. Relationships didn't work like that. "How long will you be satisfied with making do? What if these healers fail in the long run? We might not be able to mate one another without risking my life. We may never be able to have a normal sex life. That wouldn't be fair on you."

"I am happy having you at my side. It's enough."

"It's not enough," she pushed.

"I am sure they will be able to develop a contraceptive. Positive even. You might not even develop clutch sickness, I'm not a Feral male, have you considered that? I'm not saying we should try for young or take risks with your life, but—"

"We are already taking risks with my life and that's exactly what you are saying," she half-yelled. "I'm sorry." She put up a hand. "I did not mean to shout."

"It's fine. You're worried. After what just happened, I understand and I agree, no more sex until we figure this thing out."

"I'm not just worried, I'm petrified." Cordia realized the extent of her fear with a start. She'd been so excited about being with Stone and making the trip to the lair, that she hadn't even realized how scared she was about taking this step. How fear mounted every time he spilled his seed inside her. She slid off the bed.

"I'll make us some breakfast," Stone announced. "Why don't you go and relax in the tub? We can talk about it some more later." His phone next to the bed vibrated with an incoming call.

They both turned to look. Cordia turned back, she shook her head. "There is nothing to talk about." She felt numb. Completely bewildered. She could see he was upset but at the same time, he was so blasé about everything. Ultimately, Stone had no idea. None!

"I *do* think we need to talk it through some more. It is clearly very upsetting to you, and with good reason. As long as you know I am okay with waiting as long as it takes until Meghan develops a contraceptive that works for us."

"What if it doesn't happen?" Her eyes filled with tears, but she blinked hard, holding them back.

"Of course it will happen, Cordia." Stone also stood up, standing in front of her, imploring her with his eyes. Those beautiful amethyst eyes.

"Just like you're sure there will be a cure for clutch sickness," she snapped back.

"I'm not sure of anything. All I am saying is that we should stay positive. That we can be hopeful that maybe one day—" His phone started vibrating again. Stone ignored it, didn't even look in that direction.

Cordia made her way to the closet. She put her few possessions into her bag. Her heart was heavy. It was the last thing she wanted, but it had to be done. She had been foolish to ever think this would work.

"What are you doing?" She felt Stone come up behind her. Could feel his warmth.

"This was a bad idea." She shook her head. "Us, that is." She heard his phone start up again. "You should get that."

"Screw the phone… and it's not a bad idea." He put his hands on her shoulders. "What are you saying? We just need to be more careful, that's all."

"There is no such thing as careful," Cordia turned, the tears spilling over. She wiped them away. "We've tried and it hasn't worked."

"Meghan is going to figure this out. She'll find a good contraceptive. One that will work for us." He shrugged. "It will take time but that's okay."

"And in the meantime, I could become pregnant. There is a very good chance that I will die if that happens. I might be with clutch already." She touched her belly, feeling stricken. How terrible to be so afraid of something that should be magical. It wasn't fair!

"We won't have sex. It's simple."

"We *will* have sex and you know it."

"We are intelligent adults. We can avoid having sex." He seemed unperturbed.

"And if it takes months?" She raised her brow. "Chances are good we're looking at months. It could even take years. What then?"

"We'd be okay. We'll figure it out. We really don't have to have sex but just so you know, I can scent a female in heat a mile away. I've told you that. I would know if—"

"Have you ever scented a Feral in heat?" She knew she was being hard, but someone had to be and since it was her life on the line, that person was her.

Cordia struggled to keep her memories at bay. She could still scent death. Like it had happened yesterday. Could still hear the pained screams and then later cries her sister had made for days before she had finally slipped away. It had been a blessing when it had come. Death. Enemy turned friend. It wasn't something she ever wanted to go through. She'd been right all of those years. She couldn't be in a relationship. It was something best avoided.

"You know the answer to that question. No, I've never scented a Feral in heat, but I've scented it on most other species," he lifted his eyes in thought, "other shifters, vampires, our own kind and then, humans." He nodded. "It's distinct and unmistakable. I have no doubt I would scent it on you too."

"Just like you were certain that the human coverings would work."

His phone started vibrating again. Stone didn't seem to even notice. "Maybe that was a faulty condom," he blurted. "It worked last night."

"You really believe it was faulty?" She raised her brows. "I believe the rubbers will be hit and miss, and therefore, not suitable." She shook her head.

Stone clenched his jaw before finally nodding once. "You are right. I think it might happen again."

"It will! There is too much risk involved and too many maybes." She took both his hands. "I want you to have a good life with a female who can give you everything."

"I have everything right now. I don't want anyone else." He squeezed her hands tightly.

"You say that now." She pulled in a deep breath. "I must go. I'm sorry. Before we get in too deep. Before it's too late." She tried to pull away, but he held on.

Someone knocked at the door.

"It is too late already. I'm already in too deep. I'm in love with you, Cordia. Please don't do this." He looked at her half-packed bag. "Please. I'll do anything."

"There is nothing you can do. I'm faulty... broken. There is nothing that can be done to fix me."

The person knocked again, harder this time. "Go away," Stone growled. "You are not broken," he spoke softly, keeping his eyes on hers. "We can work around this. We have each other."

She shook her head, the tears falling in earnest. "It doesn't matter how much we feel for one another. It will end in disaster. I can feel it."

"You don't—"

The door opened. Stone pushed her behind him, snarling at whoever it was that entered. "What the fuck!" he boomed, every muscle bulging.

"I'm sorry to b-bother you," a male stammered.

Cordia looked over Stone's shoulder. The male was facing the other direction. His head bowed.

"What is so damned important that you had to barge in here?" Stone's hands were curled into fists at his sides. The muscles on either side of his neck were roped.

"It's Macy... she's in trouble. Sand has called for a healer. He also asked to send for you... and your female. He specifically mentioned her as well. Sand is out of his mind. The male needs you."

"What kind of trouble?"

"Oh no!" Cordia grabbed a dress out of her bag. It was the one on top. She pulled the garment over her head, handing Stone a pair of pants. He pulled them on.

"Macy is bleeding... it's bad. She's in terrible pain. The babies... it's... please, you need to come."

Stone began walking even before the male finished talking. Cordia followed him. She couldn't leave now. Not like this.

CHAPTER 18

Fuck!
  Shit!
  Holy fucking shit!

His heart pounded. His palms felt sweaty and his mouth felt dry. Cordia took a few jogging strides until she was in step beside him.

"Are you going to stay?" His voice broke slightly.

She nodded. "For now." Cordia sounded and looked completely together.

"Thank you." He took her hand in his. He couldn't deal with her leaving just then. Not with Macy in trouble.

"What else do you know about what's going on? Did Sand say anything else? Did you see Macy?" Stone asked Basalt, who was walking ahead of them.

The male glanced back, his face grave. "I don't know anything else." He shook his head. "I tried to call you a couple of times to warn you I was on my way. When you didn't answer, I ran as fast as I could. I'm sorry I barged in, but… I had to get the message to you."

"I understand and… I was busy." He tried to keep the growl out of his voice as he said the last. Tried not to think about the conversation he and Cordia had been having before they were interrupted. He couldn't right then. There was a big part of him that was pissed at her. One snag in the road and she was ready to throw in the towel. Stone realized that she'd spent many years running and hiding. It was her go-to method of dealing with her problems. It was a cycle he would have to find a way to break if he was going to hold onto her. Maybe she just didn't love him in the way that he loved her. Maybe after all this time and all she had witnessed, it just wasn't possible. Was Cordia too closed off? Were her emotions crippled from fear?

Stone shoved all of those thoughts aside and followed Basalt into Sand and Macy's chamber. He could hear Macy moaning softly.

Stone let go of Cordia's hand and ran into the room. Meghan and Druze were there. The doctor was taking Meghan's blood pressure.

Sand looked up, his face was pale. His eyes wide and filled with worry. "You came." He glanced from him to Cordia, returning his eyes to his female.

"Of course," Stone growled. "What happened?"

Macy lay on the bed. She was clutching her belly, her face pulled tight with pain. Her eyes squeezed shut.

"Mace fainted." Sand finally pulled his gaze off Cordia, looking back at him. His friend exhaled roughly. "She was bleeding when she woke up. The pain is worse… much worse."

"Worse?" Stone frowned. "We were here last night. Macy seemed fine. We had dinner. We laughed… we had a good time."

"I know. My female has been having pains." Sand looked down. "I knew they were worse than she was letting on. She said it was normal. We thought it was normal." He glanced down at his mate.

"Minor pain," Meghan began, "discomfort is probably a better word to use – is normal. The pain should not have been anything more than an irritation, however."

"It's been getting worse," Macy moaned the words. "I didn't want to believe anything was wrong. I was so sure it was just my ligaments stretching. I thought it was more severe," she grunted, "because it's twins and progressing more rapidly than a human pregnancy. I swear," she pushed out a breath, "I would never risk my babies. If I knew—" She groaned.

"Shall I make up a draught for the pain?" Druze asked, looking concerned.

"Not just yet," Meghan answered him. "Where exactly does it hurt?" She directed her attention back to Macy. "Is it all over your stomach area or more to one side?"

"It hurts here." She held her hand over the right side of her belly.

"Lie on your back, please. I'm going to palpate the area. Tell me if you can't take it."

Macy nodded, moving to lie on her back. She winced as Meghan began to apply pressure.

"What is it?" Stone half-yelled. "What's wrong?"

Meghan frowned. "It's hard to tell."

"Hard to tell what?" Sand asked. "What is it, Meghan? Please!"

Macy moaned.

"Do you have any pain in your shoulder or in this region?" Meghan touched her gently.

Macy shook her head, wincing. She continued to clutch her belly. "My babies… This is bad, isn't it?"

"I'm afraid it may be, based on your symptoms," the doctor continued. "Slightly low blood pressure, dizziness and fainting, abnormal vaginal bleeding and pelvic pain. You also have endometriosis, which is a definite cause of the diagnosis I have in mind. You can make that draught." Meghan instructed Druze, who nodded once and walked to the back of the room.

"Macy was treated for her condition though," Sand said.

"I know." Meghan nodded. "But it is cited as one of the causes of ectopic pregnancy."

"What is that?" Sand asked, he kept looking at Cordia, who was standing just behind him.

"It's when the embryo, or in this case embryos, implant and begin to grow in the fallopian tube instead of in the uterus. Based on the location of the pain, I'm quite sure it's your right tube that's affected. The fallopian tube carries the egg to the uterus. It is not designed to grow a baby to maturity."

"No, that can't be," Macy groaned. "Please don't say it. It can't. It just can't!"

"We would need an ultrasound to correctly diagnose you. As you know, that's not possible. We already tried to give you one and there was nothing to see. I suspect it's the hCG in the blood that makes the uterus impenetrable to ultrasound waves when a female is pregnant with a species child."

"So what now?" Sand asked, expression tense. "How

do we fix it?"

"Macy's fallopian tube is being damaged by the growing embryos. The pregnancy cannot be allowed to progress. Her lowered blood pressure concerns me, as it is an indication of internal bleeding. I suggest operating to remove—"

"No… my babies… you can't… please," Macy begged, tears streamed down her face.

"I'm sorry." Meghan smoothed the hair from her face. "I am almost one hundred percent sure of my diagnosis. Your fallopian tube may be irreparably damaged if I don't operate right away. I'm not a gynecologist but I do feel I'm capable of performing the surgery. I don't suggest that you wait. This is an emergency. The most we can hope for is that one of the embryos implanted in the uterus and that there is only one is in your fallopian tube, however, I don't hold much hope. This has progressed too rapidly."

"Surely you can move them to where they should be?" Sand asked, looking anguished.

"I'm afraid not." Meghan shook her head, her eyes were filled with pity. "That's not how this works. The embryos are too delicate for such a surgery. I will need to remove either one or both embryos immediately. I must move you to my rooms and prep for surgery. Thankfully, we do have all the necessary equipment. I will call my assistant right away."

"No! You can't! I won't let you!" Macy shouted.

"You could die if I don't perform the surgery," Meghan stated, looking Macy in the eyes. "At best, you would survive but you would lose function of one of your ovaries. You could even be rendered infertile. That's the best-case scenario."

Sand kept looking at Cordia. Why was he staring at his female?

"I don't care!" Macy pushed out. "Don't hurt them, please."

"I'm sorry to have to tell you but with the way you are bleeding, they are probably gone already or will be very soon." Meghan's whole stance had softened. Her eyes were filled with empathy.

"No." Macy pushed her head into the pillow and wailed.

Sand was completely distraught. A tear rolled down the male's cheek.

Fuck! Stone didn't know what to do or to say. This was a mess.

Sand looked up, eyes locking with Cordia's once again. He seemed to be imploring her with his eyes. *Why? What was going on?*

Cordia stepped forward and cleared her throat. "I am a Feral," she stated.

Stone blinked at the admission. *Why had she said that?* Everyone was aware of the fact.

Sand seemed relieved. *Why?* He even sighed, his shoulders slumping forward.

"We have healing capabilities." Cordia pushed out a breath, looking unsure of herself. "Unfortunately, our power is limited. I've used most of my healing energy."

"What?" Stone shook his head. "I didn't know."

"It never came up." Cordia glanced his way before looking back at the distraught couple.

"Could you try to help my mate?" Sand widened his eyes. "Please. I would be forever in your debt."

"I wish I could. I don't know if it's possible. I will try. I'm sure I used all of my power already… most of it. If the situation is as bad as it sounds…" She stopped talking. "Let's wait and see," she finally added. "I will do my best." She nodded, looking worried. Her mouth was tight. Her eyes had worry lines around them. She was frowning deeply.

Druze brought the draught over to Macy. It was a brown liquid in a small, glass cup.

"Please don't give her anything… not yet," Cordia requested. "I'm sorry you are going through this, Macy." Her eyes softened.

"Thank you." Macy was still crying softly. Her eyes filled with pain.

"I don't think I will be able to help you." Cordia blinked a few times and sniffed. "I promise to do my best."

Macy nodded.

"I'm going to step outside to call my assistant," Meghan spoke to Sand. "Just in case the surgery is necessary."

"Yes. Do." The male looked completely shell-shocked. Sand was pale. He looked sick. He reached down and clutched his female's hand once again.

"I am going to put my hands on you, Macy. You might feel warmth. You might feel tingling. It is normal."

Macy nodded.

"Lie very still," Cordia said as she put a hand on Macy's belly. It was where the stricken woman had been clutching seconds earlier. Her face became pinched, her breathing elevated. Within seconds a vein distended on her forehead and sweat beaded on her brow. She slowly took her hand away.

"Your hand was warm," Macy sounded animated.

"Very warm. The pain was less… much less."

"And? Did you heal my female?"

Just then Macy doubled over with pain. She groaned hoarsely, squeezing her eyes shut.

"I'm sorry." Cordia shook her head. She swallowed and licked her lips. "I haven't tried to heal her yet. I wanted to see what the problem was and to test my resources. I have such little power left. Almost nothing. The healer…" She looked at the door, where Meghan was just walking back in. "You were right, healer. Both of the growing young are in the wrong place. They are both still alive. You are bleeding inside, Macy. It will only get worse."

Macy cried harder. "They're still alive, Sand. Our babies… Oh god."

Sand was crying openly now too. Stone didn't know what to do. "Can you help her?" he asked.

Cordia shook her head, her eyes glassy with unshed tears. "I don't think so. I hate being powerless. Watching someone die and being able to do nothing."

"You won't die, Macy." Meghan stepped in. "I will save your life. I am sure we can repair the damage, and in time you can try again. I know it's not what you want to hear. I know it's devastating news. I wish it could be different."

Sand and Macy held each other. They cried openly. Druze stepped away, giving them space.

"If you will let me, I will try to heal you now." Cordia took a step towards them. "I doubt it will be effective but I can, at least, give it my best shot."

"We need to get Macy into surgery. The damage to her tube is getting worse by the second."

"It wouldn't take very long," Cordia said.

"Please try," Macy choked out.

Meghan nodded once. "Okay, but I can't give you much time."

Sand moved away and Macy rolled onto her back. Her lip quivered. Her eyes were red-rimmed, and tear-soaked. She held onto Sand's hand like a lifeline.

Cordia put her hand back on Macy's stomach. Her eyes were wide and focused – more internally than externally focused, Stone realized. Her breathing turned ragged. Her face went red. Within half a minute she began to shake with exertion.

"This can't wait anymore," Meghan interjected. "I'm sorry but we have to get Macy into surgery now."

"No!" Cordia put up a hand. "Give me a minute. Don't interrupt!"

Macy groaned, pulling herself into the fetal position.

"You are out of time." Meghan shook her head. "This is all a bunch of mumbo jumbo," she added, looking stressed.

"Please, let her try one more time," Sand interjected, his face a mask of pain. "Please," he added, turning back to Macy.

"Okay, but we're now out of time." Meghan didn't sound happy at all.

Cordia put her hand back on Macy's belly and went through the motions all over again. A minute later and her hand vibrated so badly she struggled to keep it in place. Sweat dripped from her brow, making her hair stick to her forehead.

Meghan was just stepping forward and pulling in a breath when there was a bright flash of light. It was blinding. It happened so quickly that Stone wasn't sure it had even happened. Maybe he imagined it.

Cordia fell to the ground in a heap. She was out cold.

"Cordia!" Stone yelled. He dropped to his knees and cupped her cheeks. "Cordia," he tried again. It didn't take long for her eyes to move beneath her lids. Then she cracked open her eyes slightly.

"I'm okay," she whispered. "Mace… Macy." She heaved a breath, trying to open her eyes.

Yeah! Of course! Macy! Stone looked up. She was sitting up. Sand had his arm around her. "How are you feeling?" The male tucked a stray strand of hair behind her ear. "What just happened?"

"I don't know." Macy looked down at herself, her mouth falling open. "I feel better."

"You're not." Meghan shook her head. "I don't know what just happened either, but there is no way you are feeling better, and now I have two patients instead of just one." She gestured to Cordia who was trying to sit up. She looked drunk.

"No." Macy shook her head. She smiled broadly. "I feel fine. I feel better than fine."

"You need that surgery. I don't care how you feel," Meghan warned.

"No." Sand choked out a laugh. "No…" He hugged Macy. "The Feral are healers. They have powers. I know how unbelievable that sounds, but it's true." He looked down at Cordia who looked marginally better. "Thank you! Thank you so much." Then he sobered. "The babies." He took a breath. "Are they…? Are they…? Please tell me they're okay."

"They are fine." Cordia smiled. "I moved them. That's why it was so taxing. I didn't have to just heal Macy, I had to move the babies too. All is well." Cordia nodded once, blinking slowly, like talking was too much for her.

"Oh my god!" Macy yelled. "I can't believe it. Thank you, Cordia!"

"We owe you everything. Name it!" Sand boomed.

Stone helped Cordia up, putting an arm around her.

"I…" Meghan looked skeptical. She put her hands on her hips.

"Didn't you see the light? It was bright. If you blinked, you might have missed it," Sand asked Meghan.

"I saw something but…" The doctor looked deep in thought.

"It's true," Druze said. "I also heard something about the Feral. I saw the light. You can see how Macy's color has improved. I'm sure if you took her BP again it would be improved too."

"My mate is fine. Our young…" Sand choked out a laugh. He was smiling broadly, a tear tracked down his cheek. "Our little boys are going to be just fine."

"I've never been so happy in all my life." Macy cupped Sand's cheeks. "I love you so much."

"I could have lost you." Sand put his arms around Macy and pulled her in close.

"By the way…" Cordia pulled herself away from him as she stood fully upright. Stone was happy to see that she was looking much better. She frowned, looking confused. "You are having a male and a female."

"What?" Sand gave his head a shake. His expression grew quizzical. "That's not possible. I'm afraid you are wrong, Cordia. When species and humans pair, we only ever have males. It has never been any other way."

"That would explain it." She spoke more to herself. "One of the young was changing…" She looked up, like she was struggling to come up with the right terminology. "The growing... what was it that you called it, healer? Something with an E."

"Embryo."

"That's it." Cordia nodded. "The one embryo was a female, but it was changing... becoming... It was evolving into a male. It seemed wrong, so I corrected the abnormality. It didn't take much energy, or I would have left it."

"So," Meghan was contemplative, "the genetic make-up was somehow altering. That doesn't seem possible and yet—"

"And yet," Sand interjected, "all of our young have been male, so it makes sense. Maybe the Feral community can help us overcome this problem. Not just us, all of the species."

"A pigeon pair." Macy chewed on her bottom lip, her eyes bright.

"A female," Sand breathed the word. "The first to be born in many years."

"Two healthy children." Macy punched him lightly on the arm.

"Of course." Sand brushed his lips against Macy's. The female suddenly looked exhausted.

"Call me if the pains return," Meghan said, clearly not convinced.

"I'll be fine." Macy smiled. "I just need to rest."

"We're having a male and a female!" Sand yelled. "Two healthy babies," he quickly added with a laugh.

Meghan smiled and shook her head. "Call me." She left, Druze following behind. He lifted his hand in farewell.

"I'm so glad it all worked out." Cordia smiled as well.

She looked at Stone. "You can help me till I can stand a little better, please."

"I mean it. Anything you want. I can never repay you," Sand said.

"I don't need anything." Cordia smiled. "I'd love to babysit the children sometime. That will be reward enough."

"Anytime! The two of you can be godparents to the babies," Macy blurted.

"You don't have to give an answer just yet. Not that you and I have discussed that yet, sweetheart." Sand widened his eyes at Macy.

Cordia giggled softly. "We'll leave you now. You do look tired, Macy. Rest would be good." She yawned herself.

"You also need to rest." Stone kept his arm around Cordia. "You have dark smudges under your eyes, which," he looked closer, "come to think of it, are red-rimmed. Let's go." He looked back at Macy and Sand. "I'm glad things worked out. Congrats on the pigeon pair. Oh, and about that gift I bought—"

"What gift?" Macy asked.

"I'll explain later," Sand said, his eyes moving back to Stone. "What about it?"

"I'm going to have to get another one. I bought baby blankets and they're both blue. That won't work anymore." Stone smiled. "I'm going to have to buy pink."

"Pink." Macy beamed.

"I still can't believe it."

They said their goodbyes. Stone couldn't believe it either. There were so many things he didn't know about this female.

CHAPTER 19

"You were right about being open-minded," Cordia blurted as they walked back to Stone's nest.

"No," Stone shook his head. He was scowling. "You were right about being ultra-cautious."

"No!" Cordia shook her head. "*You* were right. Your healers are very good. Meghan knew exactly what was wrong with Macy. She doesn't even have any powers. That's amazing. What else do these healers know? What can they do? I'm very impressed. I was doubtful but… I changed my mind."

"Um…" Stone looked skeptical. "I beg to differ. You are the one who healed Macy. Not Meghan or Druze. It was you. You didn't even need a scalpel and an operating room to do it. That was incredible. *You* are incredible." He stopped walking, putting his arms around her. "I'm in awe of you." He hugged her tighter.

Cordia enjoyed the moment for a time before pulling

back. "Thank you. I appreciate the kind words, but you were right about human healers. I'm glad I was able to use my power." She felt such joy. Such happiness. "I didn't have much left, but it worked. It worked! I almost couldn't believe it. You were right, different species can help one another. It *is* possible. We can help each other more than we can help our own. Working together, we are stronger."

"I didn't even know you had powers of healing." His eyes were wide and filled with interest.

"I don't anymore." She licked her lips. "I wasn't sure there was enough left. There almost wasn't." She rubbed her face. "I tried hard to save my sister. I used up most of my power then. I was sure I could do it. I thought that if I tried harder. Dug deeper. Even when I knew it wouldn't work, I still tried. Our powers don't work on our own kind and because Macy is a different species, it worked on her. Different species are good for one another. *We,*" she took his hands in hers, "are good for one another."

Stone shook his head. "Watching what happened to Macy… seeing Sand." He widened his eyes, which turned glassy. "I can't ever go through that with you. Macy could have died. I've been too… casual about your problem." He sniffed, biting down for a second on his lower lip. "I love you too much, Cordia." He took her hands. "I have put your life at risk. I'm so sorry. I'm an idiot! A jerk! I don't ever want to see you hurting."

"You weren't necessarily wrong in your thinking. I realize that now. I think you might be on to something. Maybe we *do* need to keep an open mind."

"No!" He shook his head, his purple eyes becoming turbulent and dark. "No sex until we are sure you are safe. Not even once. I'm okay with never having kids. I agree, we should resign ourselves to that. I can't have you in a situation like that… or worse. Your safety is my number one priority. Even hearing you say you were leaving…" He squeezed her hands. "That terrified me. The thought of not having you in my life scares the crap out of me. We're not taking any chances. From here on out it's you and me… just the two of us. You're enough for me because you are everything to me."

Cordia felt her throat clog. She felt her eyes sting. "You are everything to me as well. I love you too… very much. I'm okay with it just being the two of us."

"I wish I could mate you right now." Stone put his forehead to hers for a beat or two.

Cordia looked around them. There were several people walking down the hallway they were in. "Right now? That might be a bit awkward."

"I wasn't being literal." Stone laughed. "You know what I mean."

"We technically only just met. It's probably a good thing that we are forced to wait. I know I want to spend forever with you," she shrugged, "so what does it matter?"

"You're right." He brushed his lips over hers.

Cordia felt content. She felt complete. Her life felt full. Her future too.

CHAPTER 20

Three weeks later…

Cordia clutched the bedcovers, hearing them rip. She didn't care right then. Couldn't! Not with Stone's tongue laving on her clit. Not with two… maybe even three of his fingers inside her. Not with his thumb… A deep groan was drawn from her as her snatch began to spasm. She made some sort of garbled noise. A mix between her own tongue and English.

Her male knew how to get her there and – more importantly – how to keep her there. *Right there*. Holding her… holding… holding before slowly allowing her to come down. Her head tilted back. Her breathing was ragged. Instead of being boneless and completely sated, a need began to grow inside her all over again.

This male. He did things to her. Maybe because they still hadn't been able to mount. That could be it. Had to be.

Cordia rocked against his hand. She wanted more. No, needed it. "What do you say we 69? I would love to suck on your prick." She stretched out before pulling herself up onto one elbow.

Stone licked his lips, looking just as sated, even though he had not found release. "Let's have breakfast first. Then I definitely—"

Cordia shook her head. "You've been over-feeding me, my dresses—"

Her phone rang. She ignored it.

"You should get that. It's the third time that person has tried to contact you in the last few minutes."

"Really?" She smiled. "I didn't hear a thing." Then she grimaced. "We really need to put our phones on silent when we're in bed… or in the shower… or the bath… When we're fooling around." She winked at Stone, who laughed.

"Yeah, our phones would be off a lot of the time."

"That's true." She laughed with him.

"Get that, please!" Stone urged when her phone started up again.

"Fine, but I'm on top when we 69."

"I wouldn't have it any other way." Stone kissed her palm before placing her phone in her hand.

"Hi," Cordia said as she swiped to answer.

"Finally," Vicky pushed out a breath. "What took you so long?"

"I'm sorry. I was busy." She smiled, feeling warm inside.

"I'm with clutch," Vicky squealed, sounding excited.

Cordia sat upright in bed, her heart raced. Her mind raced too. Blood seemed to rush through her veins. She could hear it in her ears, from the inside out.

"Cordia... are you still there?"

"Yes... sorry, yes," she replied. "That's great." Her voice was tense. Her whole body had tensed up.

"You don't sound like you think it's great." Her friend sounded upset more than angry.

"I'm worried, Vicky. That's all. Otherwise, I'm thrilled for you and Talon. I swear I am."

"We're thrilled. Talon is nervous. Understandably so, but I know in my heart it's going to be okay. Don't ask me how. Call it a gut instinct."

"I'm sure you're right." Worry still churned but she forced it aside. "Human doctors are very good. Our kind should consider bringing them on board to assist. We tried to go it alone before, using just our own healers and our powers and it didn't turn out very well." She shook her head. "Things have changed since then." She lay back down.

"Talon is discussing it with his superiors. The ball is already rolling, but thanks for the advice. Good to know we are on the right track."

"You're sure you're with clutch?" Cordia added. "It's not like the Feral have a test we can take or anything."

"Very sure. I've been super horny these last few weeks. As you know, that's a sign." She giggled. "I was told about it but didn't think it would affect me." She giggled some more. "Like, I can't get enough of my mate. We literally just have sex," Vicky spoke softly, "and I want more. It's nuts! My clothes are all too tight and then—"

"You felt them," Cordia whispered; she was still lying

on her back on the bed.

"Yes," Vicky gushed, sounding delighted. "You can't miss them. Three lumps inside my belly. If you have a good feel, you can just make them out. They're small right now. They're the size of a half a chicken egg."

"They'll grow. Hopefully not too big, since you have to push them out."

"Talon said that the eggshell stays semi-soft and malleable, so as to make it easier."

"That is right. Soft and yet they are really strong. You'll be fine. If a human can push out a whole baby, you can push out three eggs."

"They're big, though." Vicky laughed, sounding nervous. "The biggest part of a baby is its head. I'd say each egg will be at least that big."

"When you put it that way," Cordia bit down on her lip, "I'm worried for you for different reasons now."

"No need. I'll be fine. Oh," Vicky said, "I have another call coming in. It's Talon. I have to take this." She spoke quickly. "We need to see each other, Cordia. I want to meet your man."

"Yes… soon. I promise."

"Okay… Love you, my friend. Bye."

"Bye!" Cordia answered. Before she could say anything more, Vicky put down the phone. Cordia lay there a while, her mind working. Both worrying and feeling happy for her friend.

High sex drive.

Tight-fitting clothing.

And…

Cordia pressed on her belly gently. She used the tips of

her fingers, moving around her belly. All over... all... over.

Small but there.

Soft lumps inside.

Growing.

Her heart was pounding so hard she didn't hear Stone. He was asking her what she wanted for breakfast. Maybe he'd asked her something else. She wasn't sure. Cordia sat up. Her eyes were wide and she struggled to breathe. At least it felt that way. It was like her chest had grown tight. "Eggs," she blurted.

"Oh." Stone looked confused. "I thought you didn't eat eggs. Are you feeling okay, my love? You don't look..." He narrowed his eyes on her.

"I'm with clutch," she said again, feeling bewildered. Feeling... She burst into tears. "I'm with clutch." She put a hand to her belly, the tears coursing down her cheeks.

"Who? Your friend... Vicky? I gathered, sorry," he added. "I couldn't help but overhear your conversation."

"No..." She shook her head, trying hard to stop the tears and failing. "Not Vicky. Yes," she quickly added, "Vicky is also with clutch."

"Also...?" He frowned hard. "You're losing me here." He walked over to the bed, concern etched into his features.

"Me. It's me as well. I'm also with clutch." With that, the tears fell quicker. Her whole body shook with sheer emotion.

"That can't be." Stone dropped the hand towel he had been holding. His brow was furrowed. "I didn't scent anything. You didn't go into heat." He sat down on the bed next to her, making her bounce lightly.

"I must have." She shook her head, the tears still coming. Such incredible fear accosted her. Was she going to die? She might. There was a good chance. Maybe not, though. Maybe... *Oh, by the gods. By feather and paw.* What had she done? What had *they* done?

"No. Come on... we've been so careful. No sex at all. Not since," he swallowed hard, "soon after you arrived. That one time... when the condom broke."

"There were also a couple of times during the conference. It's possible." She sniffed, using the back of her hand to wipe her nose.

"I know but come on... unlikely." He looked shocked. His brain working.

"I can feel them," Cordia practically whispered. "Not three but two eggs. Must be because of you. Normally there are three. They're there though... inside me. I'm slightly bigger around my middle. My clothes... I blamed you for all the great cooking but..." She shook her head. "I'm..." Hot tears streamed down her face. Her nose ran. She sniffed.

"Fuck!" Stone's eyes were blazing. "I don't know how to feel. I want to be happy because having young with you would be like... unbelievable. It would make me the happiest male alive, and yet..." His jaw tensed. "If anything were to happen to you." He shook his head. "I... I'm sorry. This is my fault. What the hell are we going to do?" He jumped up off the bed.

"No, it's not your fault at all. I had sex with you willingly. I didn't even tell you I was fertile those first few times. If anything, you should be angry with me."

"No," he shook his head, "I'm a grown male. I didn't use protection. I didn't even give it a thought that first time. Then I talked you into trying the condoms. That was a mistake." He shook his head. "I can't believe this." He raked a hand through his hair.

"Let's not bring blame into this. What are we going to do? We need a plan here." Her hands were shaking. "I'm scared but there is a part of me that is excited too. I'm crazy. I should be in a full-blown panic right now."

"We 're going to get through this." He pulled out his phone. "We'll get the best medical help." He paced. "I know just the male who can help us." He kept on pacing.

"Who?" she asked.

"Druze."

The male Stone's sister had been mated to? The one who had left to have a baby with a human? The male who hadn't said more than two words a few weeks back when Macy was in an emergency situation? That male? "I'm not sure that's such a good idea."

"Druze has been on an apprenticeship with our healers since soon after my sister died."

"Your sister took her own life because of him."

"Druze has given his life over to finding a cure for our females. He was next in line for security leader. Not me! I got the role when he fell apart after Amethyst died." Stone shook his head, his eyes filled with pain. "The male was a talented warrior. Still is. Our king refused to give him leave to study to become a healer. He's been working day and night for years to get to where he is. I know that he would do anything for me. I would trust him with my life…" Stone knelt down before her, there were tears in his eyes. "I trust him with your life and the life of our whelps, which is more important by far."

Cordia felt herself smile. It was tiny. The smallest

upturning of the lips "I might not have whelps. I'm not sure what they'll be." Her smile grew, as did her fear. She managed to tamp it down but only because of the male in front of her. "Okay. I trust you, and if you trust him, then… that's what we'll do."

AUTHOR'S NOTE

Charlene Hartnady is a USA Today Bestselling author. She loves to write about all things paranormal including vampires, elves and shifters of all kinds. Charlene lives on an acre in the country with her husband and three sons. They have an array of pets including a couple of horses.

She is lucky enough to be able to write full time, so most days you can find her at her computer writing up a storm. Charlene believes that it is the small things that truly matter like that feeling you get when you start a new book, or when you look at a particularly beautiful sunset.

BOOKS BY THIS AUTHOR

The Chosen Series:
Book 1 ~ Chosen by the Vampire Kings
Book 2 ~ Stolen by the Alpha Wolf
Book 3 ~ Unlikely Mates
Book 4 ~ Awakened by the Vampire Prince
Book 5 ~ Mated to the Vampire Kings (Short Novel)
Book 6 ~ Wolf Whisperer (Novella)
Book 7 ~ Wanted by the Elven King

Shifter Night Series:
Book 1 ~ Untethered
Book 2 ~ Unbound
Book 3 ~ Unchained
Shifter Night Box Set Books 1 - 3

The Program Series (Vampire Novels)

The Feral Series

Demon Chaser Series (No cliffhangers)

Excerpt

USA TODAY BESTSELLING AUTHOR
CHARLENE HARTNADY

CHAPTER 1

Oh no!

Her shoulders slumped while her heart pounded. Vicky forced herself to maintain eye contact as Patrick walked towards her. Maybe she was reading too much into the look on his face. Maybe...

"You're broke," her accountant said, dropping a file on her desk before planting his hands on the wood surface and staring down at her.

Vicky knew her finances were bad. She hadn't realized they were quite this bad. That it had happened this fast. "Broke, as in…?" She widened her eyes, sucking in a deep breath. Maybe he was being a bit too dramatic.

His stare softened. Patrick took a seat in the chair across from her. *Oh boy!* "Broke as in, sell your wheels. Broke, as in, watch your furniture get carted away. Broke as in, you're in the minus."

"Shit!" She pulled the file closer, not opening it. "Dammit! I can't believe this. How is this possible?" She knew the answer to her own stupid, stupid question.

"You have very little revenue still coming in. The overhead on this place is through the roof."

"What about my half of the money from the sale of the house?"

"Gone. I repeat, your overhead on this place is high." He looked around them, making a whistling noise. Vicky knew exactly what he would see. A spacious, well-appointed office with a waiting room out front. There was also her personal assistant. And the view. Her magnificent view of the park. "Image is everything," she mumbled.

Patrick snorted. "You're telling me. Problem is, image costs money. All of this costs more money than what you have coming in. A lot more."

"I don't get it." Anger burned inside her. Vicky tried hard to get herself back under control and failed. Her world was crashing down around her. Just when she had started to feel marginally better. Just when she thought she could get over what that bastard had done to her. She jumped to her feet and paced to the large window, for once, not even seeing the green grass, the trees, the dogs on leads, the joggers, the ducks on the lake. None of it. "How is it that Jeff cheats on me and he's doing better than ever, while I'm on the verge of losing everything?"

"I'm so sorry, Vicky," Patrick offered. "It isn't fair."

It didn't make her feel any better. "No," she responded. "I really need to know. He lied, he cheated, he's the bastard in all of this." Her business partner – make that ex-partner. Ex-husband. He *was* her partner once though, for better or for worse. In both business and life. The Love Doctors. The two of them had been *the* couple to see. The relationship specialists. "I got to keep the name, yet, he still manages to get the clients." *The Love Doctor.* She felt like laughing. It hadn't helped her one bit. Her clients had disappeared quicker than candy a birthday party. They all went to him now.

"He's a bastard. No doubt." Patrick shook his head. "What he did to you, Vicks…" More shaking of the head.

"Why then?" Her voice broke. "How is he still in business? Moreover, how is he still thriving? I don't get it. I don't." She shrugged her shoulders once. They felt heavy. Everything inside of her felt leaden and weighted.

"He may have cheated but he ended up moving in with her. Jeff and his fiancée are very happy. At least, they look it on the surface. You said it yourself, image is everything."

Jeff and that woman were happy and it made her feel physically ill. They had the family home, the dog, the… *Arghhhh!* She couldn't think about it without getting upset. Let alone talk about it. Would it be rude if she covered her ears and started to make noises so that she didn't have to listen to any more of this?

"Kerry is starting to show." *No more, please.* "She has

that whole glowing thing going on. She's young and pretty and glowing and they make a really beautiful family. The wedding date has been moved up so that they can get hitched before the baby comes. I don't say this to hurt you, Vicky."

It *did* hurt though. Vicky bit down on her lower lip to stop it from quivering.

"I really don't." He reached over, looking for a second like he was going to clasp her hand and then thought better of it. "Point being," Patrick continued despite her discomfort, "they look happy. They paint a perfect picture. The general population would rather buy advice on love from Jeff."

"So, I'm the woman who couldn't keep her husband? There's something wrong with *me* then?" She pointed to her chest.

Patrick didn't say anything. She pulled on her ponytail, letting her fingers slide down the length of her hair. "He cheated with a woman almost ten years our junior. I left him. *I* left *his* sorry ass. It wasn't the other way around. No one knows that, do they? They don't know how he begged me to forgive him. How he got on his knees. No, they see them playing happy families and assume there's something wrong with *me*."

"It's not fair. It's really wrong and yet…" Patrick shook his head, "that's what the numbers are saying. I told you not to get that billboard. It cost more than what you had, Vicks."

"I was so sure it would work." Vicky pushed out a heavy breath. "Business has picked up."

"You needed that phone to ring off the hook. You got… what? Three, maybe four new clients?"

"More like two." She sat down on the edge of her desk, looking down at her shoes. "I really thought it would work." Stupid, stupid billboard idea. "What now? What next?"

Patrick shrugged. "If you want to try to make a go of the business, you need to drastically downscale." He looked around her office. "You can start by letting your PA go."

She sucked in a breath. "I can't do that. Maggie and Will just put a down payment on a new home. I—"

"You have no choice, Vicks." He looked at her pointedly for a few seconds, something flared in his eyes. It was a pity. Her stomach rolled.

"I would suggest filing for bankruptcy though. I don't think you can salvage your business at this stage, unless something major happens."

The blood drained from her face. Her limbs felt weak. Her mind raced. "Major like how?"

"Like a serious influx of cash – but we both know that isn't going to happen. You need to be realistic at this stage."

"I would lose everything if I filed for bankruptcy. I'm thirty-five years old, I can't lose everything I've worked so hard to build."

"You can still start over. You're resilient, someone who always lands on her feet. You are a qualified relationship therapist. You have a degree and that's got to count for something."

Vicky covered her face with her hands and huffed out a breath. "I don't think I—"

"You don't have a choice." He spoke softly, but with conviction. "File for bankruptcy, close the business, and get a job."

"How the hell do I go back to counseling couples with marriage problems? How do I possibly campaign on keeping them together when I no longer believe in love? In happily ever after?" It shocked her to hear herself say it. Yet, it made sense. It made perfect sense.

"No wonder you're struggling as a *Love Doctor.*" Patrick put on a weird voice when he said Love Doctor. "As a relationship specialist. You don't believe in love. I don't blame you though, Vicky."

"No, I guess I don't believe in love anymore. Jeff ruined that for me, big time. It's all just a farce. You're right, I need to shut this whole thing down. File for bankruptcy and…" she shrugged, "I'm not sure what my next step will be. Couples counseling though…" She shook her head. "I hated that type of counseling right off the bat. I preferred bringing people together rather than trying to keep them together."

"Why did you choose this line of work in the first place?"

"To make money. Charge by the hour and all that. I liked the idea of becoming a doctor, but blood makes me queasy. I guess," she pulled in a deep breath, trying to get her emotions under control, "I love the whole falling in love thing and I like bringing people together. At least, I used to enjoy it very much. Now I'm just jaded and cynical. I hate that." She said the last more to herself.

"It's normal to have those types of feelings. My point is that you used reason and logic to choose a career, well, mostly. That's what I've always admired about you. It's only been a year since… well… since the rug was pulled out from under you."

"If by having the rug being pulled out from under me, you mean catching my husband bonking a much younger woman, then yeah, you would be right."

Jeff, her high school sweetheart. Her first love. First everything. What stung the most was that they had just started trying for a family. Thankfully she'd found out about his lying, cheating ways before it was too late to run the hell away.

"It's only been a year. Your wounds are still fresh. It's logical that you would still be so emotional about all of this. I'm urging you to try to be rational though. To take emotion out of business decisions. What you're doing right now isn't working. You need to change tactics."

What she needed was a fresh start. Only problem was that fresh starts cost money. "You're probably right." She blew a breath out through her nose. "I wish that billboard had worked."

"Forget the damned billboard." Patrick sounded annoyed.

"Fine," she all but whispered. "I'll figure something out."

CHAPTER 2

"Here." Cadon threw an oversized loincloth at him. Talon couldn't believe humans enjoyed wearing this type of garb.

He watched as it fell at his feet. The material the color of a winter's sky. He picked the garment up. Oversized was being conservative. It was huge. Several loin cloths could be fashioned from the material. Why the need to cover so much skin? It was unnecessary.

Cadon caught his look of distaste because he chuckled. "Don't let its size fool you. Wearing that thing will be tight and uncomfortable, for sure."

"It is." Soren pulled on the material around his neck. "You'll feel like it's strangling you," he tugged at the fabric near his ass, "everywhere."

Soren and Pace laughed. Talon grunted. He still wasn't sure why Leukos had chosen him for this assignment. He pushed out a deep breath, mentally preparing for the task ahead. Probably because he was level-headed, could think on his feet and because, like the others chosen, he'd lost a mate. Which meant he wasn't looking for or interested in human females. In females, period. Back to being level-headed. At least he knew his prick wouldn't do the thinking or the talking for him. It was one small consolation.

There were days when he missed his mate terribly. Lark had been a good companion. His chest tightened for a moment. There was no time to dwell on such things, Talon pulled on the loincloth. The fabric covered both legs, all the way to his ankles. So impractical. The material was, thankfully, soft. He pulled his cock to the side, having to suck in a breath to zip the garment closed.

Good thing he no longer had any use for it because his prick felt like it was being squashed to death in there. Talon made another grunting noise, arching his back. It didn't improve things. How did humans handle this? It was terrible.

"Nothing helps." Soren was grinning. "Hopefully we will get used to the discomfort."

"I wouldn't count on it." Pace was frowning heavily.

Talon had to agree with Pace. There was no way he was getting used to this. He pulled the shirt over his head. "Are you sure these are normal human attire?" He rubbed a hand over the garment. "Why is there a picture of a bird on the front?"

"Yes, it's perfectly normal. Humans have very strange taste in things." Soren made a face. "You saw the pictures of the humans. They wear all sorts of colors." The male was trying to force his feet into tube-like things that fit around them awkwardly. Talon couldn't remember what they were called. "They are shoes," Soren announced, obviously catching his quizzical look. "Humans do not walk around much without them."

"I remember from our training. They look worse than the human loincloths," Cadon interjected, eyes wide and staring at the foot tubes.

"My feet feel squashed," Soren groaned. "This can't be right." He shook his head, looking down at his feet.

"I'll take those." They were flat rubber, with a piece that fit between the toes. Talon tested them out, feeling the rubber slap against soles of his feet with every step. It was doable though. At least his feet would be mostly free. That was something at least.

Cadon quickly snatched up the remaining rubber shoes, leaving Soren and Pace to wrestle the tubes onto their feet.

Once they were all dressed, Cadon handed each of them a bag.

"Let's go over the plan," Talon said, looking each male in the eyes, from one to the other. "Cadon, you take us through everything. You were the one who conducted the preliminary research."

Cadon nodded once. "Inside the bag is money. Humans use it to buy the things that they need. You cannot just take something. You have to give some of the money in return for an item. There is also a plastic card that has money inside it. The card can be used instead of the paper money."

"I still do not understand how such a small plastic card can have so much paper money inside of it." Soren narrowed his eyes. The male shrugged. "I guess we'll figure it out."

"Yes, we will." Cadon nodded. "There is a cellphone

with each of our numbers programmed in. We will use it to stay in contact with one another. I hope you all remember how to use it." He paused. When no one said anything, he continued. "Do not forget to charge your cell phone by plugging it into the wall."

It didn't make much sense, but Talon nodded, as did the others. Soren was right, they would have to figure it all out. "The goal is to learn as much about the humans as possible. The females are of particular importance. We need to be able to teach the others all we learn so that they will be in a better position to win one as a mate when the time comes."

"I'm not so sure it is a good idea to split up." Pace shook his head, brow furrowing.

"Neither do I," Soren said, still tugging at the fabric at his ass.

"Why don't the two of you stick together then?" Talon offered.

Pace looked at Soren, who cocked his head. "Yes, sounds good to me."

Pace nodded. "That's settled then. What about the two of you?"

Talon looked over at where Cadon was standing. The male looked at him with indifference. "I think we'll stick to the plan and spread out," Talon said. "More chance of getting somewhere with these females."

Cadon nodded. "Fine by me."

"A hotel is the name of human accommodations. Other names used are Motel and Bed and Breakfast. B and B for short," Talon reminded them. "We use the card money to pay and we can order food there as well. Find one, get settled and get started."

All three males nodded. "Now remember," Cadon cautioned, "human males are intimidated easily. All humans, for that matter, scare easily, so we need to be as unassuming and polite as possible."

"Agreed." Talon nodded. "Let's stay in contact with one another. Each of you is to check in on a daily basis," he added. "That way, we will know that everyone is safe. The two of you can contact Cadon and I will, in turn, check in with Cadon. We need to do this every day as the sun is a quarter of the way in the sky. Let's make the next six weeks count."

"I'm sure we will all be experts by the time we go back," Pace said, his voice filled with arrogance.

"I will have the females eating out of my hand in no time." Cadon grinned.

Talon cracked a half-smile. "Not with that ugly beak on you."

"Don't make me wish feather rot on you." Cadon laughed.

"We'll stay in touch." Talon bumped shoulders with the male and then did the same with the other two.

"Any ideas on where to start?" Pace had a bewildered look on his face.

Cadon shrugged. "Not even the slightest clue. You two head that way." He pointed to a treed area. "Are you happy to head in that direction?" he asked Talon, pointing to a lake.

Ducks floated aimlessly on its surface. There was a footpath just to the right of them that made its way over to the lake, joining another such path. "You can go left, and I'll go right." Cadon shrugged, like he didn't particularly care either way.

It didn't make any difference to him either. "Let's do this." Talon began to walk in that direction.

"Good luck," Cadon called after him.

Luck had nothing to do with it. He needed to find a place to settle in and then he needed to start researching. The ducks splashed and cavorted. Talon was alerted to the approach of a human by rhythmic footfalls. It was a female. She jogged towards him. This was as good a time as any. He may as well start working right now.

Her eyes flared as they landed on him. Talon smiled at her. He knew he was a big male. Especially next to most humans, but surely he could come across as friendly. The rhythm of her footfalls faltered for a moment or two before resuming.

"Excuse me," he tried to sound kind and easy-going, "can I—"

The female turned. As in pulled a one-eighty and all out sprinted in the opposite direction. He looked around him. There was no one else anywhere close to them. No one behind him. By fur and feather, he had frightened her off. In hindsight, maybe approaching a female in a deserted place was not the best way to go about things.

Talon started walking again. After just a minute or two, he broke free from the grassy area. All around him were tall towers as far as the eye could see. The ground was hard and compacted. There were several people he could see.

Another female approached him. Her hair was pinned up. Her clothing looked more form-fitting underneath the long coat she was wearing.

"Hello." He smiled at her.

The female narrowed her eyes. Her mouth tightened.

She quickened her pace, giving him a wide berth.

"I was hoping you could…" he tried again, talking to her retreating back but she kept on walking. Definitely moving much quicker than before.

He sighed. This was going to be more difficult than he had initially expected. Talon looked around him. Chaos was too casual a word. His nose twitched even though his sense of smell was not nearly as developed as the other shifters. Talon could still scent stench from the vehicles that whizzed past. The stench of human occupation. Rotting food and foul excrement. Lights blinked different colors on every corner. Many people occupied each of the towers. His jaw dropped open. Although he had seen pictures, he hadn't expected it to be quite this.

There was a loud barking to the left of him. "Hey boy!" a male shouted. Talon turned in that direction. A large dog dragged his owner, teeth bared, eyes on Talon. "Hey! Toby! Heel boy. Heel!" The male kept shouting but the dog broke free, running straight for Talon, who held his ground. He looked the small beast straight in the eyes. Very courageous for one so insignificant.

What did this measly creature think it could do against him? Teeth bared, the creature leaped towards him. Talon made a soft screeching noise from deep in his throat. A warning. The animal would get one chance. One only. The timid beast ground to an immediate halt. It's back end and tail curled underneath itself, ears flat. The animal whined as its owner ran up, grabbing its lead. "I'm sorry." He was completely out of breath. "I'm not sure what came over him." He turned to the cowering animal. "Bad dog, Toby. Bad, bad boy." He gave the animal a scratch behind the ear as he spoke. The action in complete contradiction to his tone. It confused Talon, but the beast seemed to understand. It relaxed somewhat.

Talon frowned. "No harm done." The scent of something delicious attracted him. It came from the other direction. He continued moving that way. One of the vehicles ground to a halt, its front end touching his shins.

There were a couple of loud noises that hurt his ears. The male in the vehicle was shouting something and Talon couldn't make out what he was saying at first. Then the shouting grew louder as the male stuck his head out of the vehicle. "… nuts? Are you completely out of your freaking mind?" he shouted.

Nuts. Hmmmm.

Maybe he was offering Talon food. "No, thank you," he said, trying to be polite. He didn't mind eating nuts, but they certainly weren't his favorite. Besides, he had eaten before embarking on this trip.

"I could have killed you," the male added, still screaming at the top of his lungs.

Killed. Him? That puny human? Talon tried not to laugh at the male. It wasn't nice to laugh at someone. "There is no way you could have killed me, human. Just so you know, I can hear you just fine." Talon pointed at one of his ears. He smiled at the male. Maybe he thought Talon was hard of hearing. It was nice of him to shout so loudly to ensure he could understand.

"What the…" He made a growly noise. Or tried to. Humans weren't very good at making such sounds. "Get the fuck out of the road, asshole."

Talon looked around him. Not sure what the male was trying to convey. Before he could ask what a road was, the male went on.

"Get. Out. Of the road, before I run you the fuck over." He pointed at the path Talon had just stepped off of.

Talon shrugged. He walked back to the path and the male took off, his vehicle made a loud screeching noise as it moved away, going much faster than before. They really were timid creatures.

"You could have been killed." The male with the furry creature was still there, eyes wide. The animal growled as Talon moved closer, his lip curling back from his teeth. When Talon looked down, it whined, putting its ears back and then moved behind the male's legs. "I'm not sure what Toby's problem is, he normally loves everyone."

The animal could most likely sense that Talon wasn't human. He didn't say anything to the human about it.

"You're obviously not from around here." The male raised his brows.

Talon nodded. "That would be correct." He decided not to elaborate. For the most part, they had decided to keep their non-human status quiet. If need be, they would disclose that they were shifters but nothing of their 'real' heritage.

"You can cross the road at any of the intersections." He pointed to where the bright lights at the corners were. "I would recommend that you stick to the pavement all other times."

"Pavement?" Talon looked down.

"Yep, that's right. The cars will run you over if you try to walk on the road. You could even get a ticket for jaywalking."

Talon nodded. "I will do that, thank you."

"Aren't you cold?" He looked at Talon's arms.

He shook his head, wishing he could get rid of these clothes. They were so tight and uncomfortable. So restricting.

"It must be all that muscle keeping you warm." The male wore a hat and thick garments. There was even a long, knitted piece of clothing wrapped tightly around his neck. How could the male even breathe? Talon wasn't sure how it didn't drive him mad. The human patted his animal. "Anyhow, take care. I need to get Toby home." He looked down at the beast.

"Do you have any idea where I can go to get information on females?" Talon blurted before the male could leave. It was worth a shot. Perhaps he could help him. At least he wasn't scared of Talon, which was something at least.

"Females?" He looked uncertain. "What kind of information?"

"How to meet them." Talon shrugged.

The male frowned and scratched his chin. Then he smiled. "Oh, I get it, I take it there aren't many women where you come from? That's why you're here isn't it?"

"You would be right." Talon nodded, glad that the male understood.

He looked Talon up and down. "Yeah, I see what you mean about needing some help. Maybe *she* can help you." He pointed at a big board. It was tall and wide and perched high.

There was a smiling female on the board. She looked kind and friendly and yet, sad somehow. Something he read in her eyes.

"She's a Love Doctor." The male laughed. "It says right there that she can teach you everything you need to know about the opposite sex."

Sounded perfect.

"That's her office right there." He pointed to glass doors. "Or you could send her an email or contact the 800 number supplied."

"I'll go and see her." He felt something in himself ease. "I'm sure she will be able to help me," Talon added. Besides, what other options did he have?

CPSIA information can be obtained
at www.ICGtesting.com
Printed in the USA
LVHW032014081019
633405LV00003B/1114/P